COUNTING
FOR THUNDER

Visit us at www.boldstrokesbooks.com

Counting
for Thunder

by
Phillip Irwin Cooper

2019

COUNTING FOR THUNDER
© 2019 BY PHILLIP IRWIN COOPER. ALL RIGHTS RESERVED.

ISBN 13: 978-1-63555-450-2

THIS TRADE PAPERBACK ORIGINAL IS PUBLISHED BY
BOLD STROKES BOOKS, INC.
P.O. BOX 249
VALLEY FALLS, NY 12185

FIRST EDITION: MAY 2019

CREDITS
EDITOR: JERRY L. WHEELER
PRODUCTION DESIGN: STACIA SEAMAN
COVER DESIGN BY TAMMY SEIDICK

Acknowledgments

Sincerest gratitude to Amity Janow for her initial approach, and all that came with it. Heidi Fisher, Phil Done, and Marsha Oglesby, who read early drafts. Ellen Raff, Kurt Donaldson, and Paul Hardister for holding the C4T world together with two Dixie cups, a string, and a whole lot more. Most generous agent Malaga Baldi. Editors Jerry Wheeler and Leslie Wells. Donna Ekholdt, who keeps pushing. Luis De Castro for all the previews.

For Jason Howard, who opened the window.

PROLOGUE

When I was seven years old, I had a jet-black rooster. I'd raised it and three others just as dark from baby chicks for a school project. Although he was born with some delicate distinction I could never put my finger on, I soon discovered I could tell him apart from the others by picking him up and looking him square in the eyes. There was a dash of white smack-dab in the middle of the left lens. I tied a piece of blue string around one of his legs so I could more easily identify him from a distance.

Entering the pen at feeding time one day, I noticed, to my horror, a shriveled leg next to the food bin. My second-grade mind had failed to deduce that a young rooster's leg will continue to grow, string or no string. And if said string is never loosened, the results could prove catastrophic. My blemish-eyed rooster wobbled confusedly next to my work boot, weak, staggering, and possibly near death. I called to my mother, who was gathering bed sheets from the clothesline.

"My goodness," she said, entering the pen and kneeling next to the ailing bird. Brushing the palm of her hand over the back of its head, she gathered the woozy rooster in her arms and exited the coop, disappearing into a dense patch of cedars.

An anguished hour passed before I heard the familiar strains of "Bringing in the Sheaves." My mother came into view on the other side of the garden shed, my beloved rooster following close on her heels as if he'd been born with only one leg. "We shall come rejoicing," my mother sang as she went into the pen, crouching with her back to me. She whispered words of such secrecy I could only make out a faint "de-vine."

Patting the rooster on the plume of its tail, she left the pen, closed the gate behind her, and guided me up the path. I looked over my shoulder at my rooster chasing the others away from the fresh pile of scratch my mother had left. I watched her closely as she stooped to retrieve the basket of laundry, the words of the hymn still nimbly on her lips. Ignoring my plea for any scrap of information on what had transpired between the two of them, she kicked open the door of the wrought iron gate and continued on to the house.

Trying to keep up in the wake of recent events, I seriously pondered what a sheave was, and why rejoicing always followed the bringing in of them.

1

The day I got the call my nonsmoking mother was diagnosed with inoperable lung cancer began with a trip to buy bras. Frances Newman was one of the rottenest stars in movies, and I was her chief executive assistant, which just meant I kissed more ass than anyone else for the same amount of money.

"Oh, hi, Phillip. You must be here for Ms. Newman's—"

"Bras. Right."

The pasty-faced bra ladies in the Beverly Hills boutique ask the same thing every time, even though I've never bought anything here *but* bras.

The skinny bra lady always has something wildly inappropriate to say, as if all us lowly ass-kissers should be able to let it all hang out over the counter. "So, is she an even bigger bitch now that she's won the Oscar?"

"I'm sure I don't know," I say with a strained smile, handing over Frances's black Amex, checking my imaginary watch like I had somewhere to be yesterday.

"How's the acting—or was it writing—thing going?" the heavy bra lady asks me. She had actually seen a terrible play I'd written for a none-too-reputable theatre company in the Valley.

"Oh, it's going," I say briskly as I gather the bags. Ducking into the blast of a Santa Ana pushing its way through rush hour traffic, I am suddenly overcome with the suspicion that the present nettlesome moment won't hold a candle to what's coming next.

❖

"*Us Weekly* is here and Frances is pissed." Piper, Frances's nauseatingly frisky junior assistant, greets me as I enter the front door of the manse. "Did you get the…" she says, peeking inside the glimmering bag of bras. "—Thank God. What about the corgi?"

Frances was known in her circle as the Queen of Gifting. When you work for the Hollywood elite, much of your time is spent finding the perfect gift for the person who has everything. Your days become a never-ending quest for something no one in their right mind would ever wish for.

"No corgis."

"What do you mean, no corgis?"

"I mean there's not a chocolate-covered corgi anywhere in L.A. Chocolate-covered pugs, yes. Dachshunds, yes. I was told by Merva at Sweet Chic that most consider corgis too British."

"Too *British*? For what?"

"Or Irish. Hell, I don't remember. All I know is I'm done looking for chocolate dogs." It takes an effort for a control freak like me to admit defeat, but there you have it.

"Is there anything I can report to her about the chastity belt?"

Frances's best friend, Jules, got knocked up every time she went to Paris. So, Frances thought it would be a riot to find one of the original chastity belts. "Like Anne Boleyn, or somebody like that, had to wear," she had said. This way, not only would it be a great gag, but it would be a gag worth tens of thousands of dollars.

"I finally heard from Jake at Trinity. After some digging, he found there never really were chastity belts."

"What? Of course there were. There *had* to be!"

"They only appeared in drawings in the sixteenth century. Like in cartoons. Chastity belts were a myth."

"Holy shit. We're dead."

Nearing forty and already packing enough botulism to give her the skewed smile of a stroke victim, Frances swoops through the foyer and grabs me by the shoulders. "There is a *shithole* magazine here."

"Yeah," I say flatly.

"Why don't I know this?" she hisses like a saw-scaled viper.

"I told you yesterday, and it's on your phone. It's also on the Things to Do Today list," I say, pointing to the hot pink pad on the foyer table.

Frances studies the short, dumpy reporter standing alone in the living room, picks at one of her overgrown lips, and looms close enough to French me. "*Did you get the bras?*"

I brandish the bag with a big, fake smile.

Frances grabs me in a big, brittle hug. "If you run my life forever, I will give you a big fat fucking raise every fucking year!" she squeals before she dashes away to greet the reporter in a key three octaves higher than her normal speaking voice. "Heeeey, I'm Frances."

The cell phone vibrates in my shirt pocket—Burberry button-down, a gift from Frances for remembering to bring double dressing for her salad from the Ivy on my first day of work.

"Hi, it's Cynthia," my agent's assistant says through the faulty headgear that always makes her sound like she's in the can. "Could you come over when you get a sec?"

In the living room, Frances blabs away at the reporter. "I'm just so thankful I get paid to do what I love."

❖

"What do you mean, you're letting me go?" I say.

Cynthia, an unpleasant, ruddy-faced woman in her twenties,

pops a thick rubber band on her wrist. "It's just business. And besides, it wasn't my decision. It was Gary's."

I can hear my agent's tired, pinched voice making deals through the closed plywood door. "Per diem" something something and "contracts no later than." I clutch a man purse to my chest like a bulletproof vest, something I do when I have to talk with someone who uses phrases like "contracts no later than." The bag is made of rattlesnake skin, a gift from an old girlfriend who worked as a producer on a soap opera and threw up every morning before she left for work. In the bag is a writing pad for taking notes, a Montblanc pen given me by said girlfriend, and an empty tin of Sucrets. Tucked in the side pocket is a headshot and résumé, although I haven't worked as an actor since 1997 when I had a six-day stint on *Days Of Our Lives* playing a waiter who died in a hospital explosion.

"But he just signed a two-year contract with me, and that was only two months ago," I whine, sounding more like a four-year-old who shit his pants.

"He decided he didn't have the time to build a career for someone who—" She stops herself self-consciously and pops the rubber band.

I lean forward. "Someone who *what*?"

"Well, someone who's not so young anymore. Someone who's not so young anymore and hasn't yet gotten their big break."

I wait to see if she's gonna say it again, just in case I failed to hear it the first two times. "Why didn't Gary tell me?"

"He's got a lot going on." Cynthia pops her wrist with the rubber band, and I notice dried blood around the ragged cuticles of her gargantuan, ape-like thumbs.

Gary's voice trumpets a "Fair enough!" from underneath the door.

"Oh, and before I forget…" Cynthia rummages around a desk drawer before she forks over a well-worn DVD of a film Frances made when she was less than nobody. "I've been meaning to ask if could you could get Frances to sign this for my niece. She's a fan."

❖

A Big Blue Bus craps a load of blue-black smoke in my face as my cell sings Blondie's "The Tide Is High," and I fold into my car. I answer without checking who it is. "Yup."

Like burning acid on my face. "Bo Skeet?" My childhood nickname. From my father. "It's me. Sis." Born Hannah. Again, my father's work.

"Oh. Hey, Sis. Listen, can I call you back?"

"No. You'll get busy, and I won't hear back from you for a week." The gentle hum of the potbellied filter tells me she's pacing by the pool at my parents' place.

"Not true," I mumble. "I'll call you in, like, later." I let down the window, the old roll-down kind, cursing myself for deciding it was too costly to fix the air conditioner.

"It's Tina," she exhales, like someone on a Brazilian soap opera.

"What about Tina?"

"She has cancer."

I stick a finger in my other ear to hear over Wilshire Boulevard traffic. "What??"

"Lung cancer." I can hear Sis exhaling her Carlton 100 as I light up one of my own.

"Lung cancer? Come on, Tina doesn't smoke."

"It's stage four, and it doesn't look good."

My mother had smoked one cigarette in her entire life. She had planned taking up the habit to take off a few postnatal pounds, but the day she chose to start wound up being the same day the surgeon general's first report on the dangers of smoking came out.

I hunker down in the car seat, trying to disappear. "So—come on, here—stage four. What does that mean?"

I can hear the tip of the Carlton fire as Sis takes another drag. "It means it's inoperable. They'll do chemo and radiation and hope it buys her a little time. Maybe three months."

"Three…" I say, fingering the tattered leather on the steering wheel cover.

"You'd never know it to look at her. Dot Grant followed us out of the Delchamps the other day. 'Lookin' at y'all is like lookin' at the Judds, which one's the mother, which one's the daughter?' And that fat-ass son of hers with the weird eye lookin' at me like I'm some sort of chocolate fudge Popsicle."

"Okay, stay with me here, Sis. How is she?"

"Don't you wanna know how *I'm* doing?"

I take a deep breath and try to make my stomach poke out the way they do in the yoga class I haven't been to in four years. "Of course. How are you?"

"I've been throwing up nonstop," Sis says, blowing her nose. "I've never felt so terrible in all—"

"I'm sorry you're throwing up."

"She wants to talk to you."

My back stiffens in panic.

"Hi." Tina's calm plantation dialect washes away Sis's anguished storm warning.

"Hi," I answer, quick, breezy.

"She's single *again*," she whispers. I can feel her turn her back to Sis. "She's just left that lovely girl she's been with for what, four years?"

Sis dated guys until she went off to college, then switched to girls. Before she switched back to guys. Then back to girls. This is a thing with the Stalworths. It's a wonder the family tree grew. None of the many wild cards in the tribe felt strongly enough about one sex or the other to identify as one or the other. This made outsiders crazy. And terrified me. Who wants to exist without an orientation? Although I'd dabbled with men a time or two, I was damned if I would make the end of the Stalworth line all my fault. My parents had worked too long and too hard to miss out on at least one wedding and one grandchild.

Tina's voice took me out of my wandering head. "She's up here every weekend to see your father to talk about whatever *they* talk about. I thought she had to work all the time. One would think you would have to in the real estate business. Well, maybe they don't have to work so hard in Pensacola."

I imagine my mother walking up the stairs to the sun porch, staring out over the hollow below her, the hardwoods tinged with the callow buds of springtime. I'm pulling lean, rickety words out of thin air. "Listen, how—"

"Are you coming home?"

A question I knew was coming.

"You know I risked my life to have you." Tina stops herself. "Sorry. You know I'm not that kind of person. I would *never*. It's just, your sister won't stop crying. And Fanny cleans any room I'm not in so she won't have to look at me. And don't even get me started on your father. Will you come home, just for a couple of days," she says, lowering her voice again, "so I can look at somebody who's not stark-raving mad?" She offers up a tiny laugh. "Do you catch the irony in this whole thing? I spend half my life in the looney box, and now *I* have to be the one who holds everybody together. A daunting task, to say the least."

I silently curse the click of my call waiting as Tina will think she's keeping me.

She clears her throat. "Is everything okay?"

I feel like I'm five years old. I desperately want someone to make it all okay, turn back the clock so I'm not old enough to have a parent die of anything beyond a bloody car wreck. "It's…Yes. I'm fine." An older tourist couple poses for a snapshot in front of Van Cleef & Arpels. I instantly hate them both for looking the picture of health.

"Your father just walked out here. He and Sis are trying to outpace each other. Just look at them, pulling their weeds. Two peas in a pod."

I picture my father standing on the bank of the creek like he always does when he has some difficult task before him, hands on his hips, shoulders straight, picking his teeth with something he's snatched off the ground. Then he joins Sis in another round of weeding. Father and daughter can cover a lawn the size of a football field like two gophers on holiday.

Tina's voice packs more urgency. "I need my buddy."

I can hear a car door slam through the receiver and Tina says "Hi" in a mock cheery tone to an unnamed visitor. My call waiting intrudes again, and I quickly blurt out, "I'll be home quick as I can." I feel myself slipping effortlessly back into control freak mode. "I'll do some research, see what I can find." I can tell Tina's attention is all on me and not on the visitor. "Okay?"

"That's really good news." I can tell she's smiling.

I would later learn both Sis and I would smoke the last cigarettes of our lives today.

I hang up, wondering how in four hot, fiery hells I can make this happen.

❖

I make my way past the laundry room in the gloomy parking garage of my apartment building and hold my nose against the cloying scent of the Garcias' grape-flavored detergent. The two-bedroom place I've had since I graduated college still falls under the rent control laws of the People's Republic of Santa Monica. Most days it feels like I may wind up like the other inhabitants of the crumbling abode: seniors whose withered hands will have to be pried from their cheap rental thresholds by the casket makers of the gentrified beachside community.

But a strange purpose is in my step as I dial Frances's number, an act that smacks of spontaneity and freedom, two things that never factor into my existence, as I never take vacations and always do as I am told.

"Piper, hey, it's Phillip. Didn't you have some friend who had cancer but ate some sort of Peruvian tree bark and got better?" Mrs. Garcia waves and smiles as she passes with another basket of fruit-flavored laundry. "Well, could you get me any and all phone numbers, websites, and email addresses?" I say, walking straight past the mailboxes since I know Tuesdays are supermarket circular day. "Oh. It's my mother. Listen. Has Frances had her vodka yet? Great. Could you put her on, please?"

❖

Agnes Roach has been my landlady since I first moved to L.A. Somewhere near eighty, she wears floral house dresses that snap up the front and slip-on house shoes made out of the same brushed corduroy as the slip-on arm protectors she keeps on her aging sofa.

The culprit, a hot pink Brother sewing machine, is stationed in the hall. Agnes smokes unfiltered Lucky Strikes and drinks Busch beer from a can and cats are *everywhere*, stalking, hissing, and napping on countertops, windowsills, and china cabinets. She cooks dinner for me every Sunday night: trout, mashed potatoes, green salad with iceberg lettuce and Wishbone dressing. Afterward, we drink ice-cold beer and watch *Touched by An Angel* on her prehistoric Magnavox.

As today, Friday, is the day of my departure, Agnes insists I have my last supper with her. Presently, I am finishing off a piece of Marie Callender's strawberry pie while Agnes pours Diet Squirt from a noisy plastic bottle into my Flintstones jelly glass. Agnes has always liked the fact that I feel comfortable enough to conduct business from her dinner table. Although tonight would be no different than any other at first glance, the alternative medicine book on the empty chair next to me tells a different story.

"Wait. Piper. So, is it like a spa or what?" My mind momentarily shuts down as I shoo a mewing Siamese kitten from my plate. "No, I'm at my landlady's. No, it's just a cat of some sort," I say, logging more info on my laptop.

Agnes sits in a chair at the other end of the table and plants her beer on the brushed blue corduroy tablecloth. "If your flight's at eleven, I need to go fire up the Nova." Agnes expels a breathy "Who? Me?" at the tinny *bing* of the doorbell.

"Want me to get it?" It's a tad late for visitors.

"You stay put." Agnes lumbers over to the door and calls through the peephole like a mob boss. "Who's there?"

A familiar female voice comes from the other side. "It's me, Agnes."

Agnes stands firm. "Well, I don't know who 'me' is."

"Caroline."

"Caroline with a long 'i'?"

"Yup."

Agnes's voice softens. "Lord," she says, opening the door. The yellow porch lightbulb illuminates the girl I've been seeing now for six years. "Land sakes," Agnes says, embracing Caroline, "come on in here." Caroline follows Agnes into the living room and pushes a thick strand of her long, stunning mane over one ear. Agnes grabs Caroline by the forearm and turns her to me like she's the next item up for auction. "I thought y'all was busted up."

Truth was, we were. "Well…"

Caroline smiles at Agnes, then at me. "I thought if you still needed a ride to the airport…"

"Oh, goodness," Agnes barks, "you know I am *loath* to drive after dark. Specially since those fuckers who did my laser surgery *murdered* my night vision."

I nod thankfully at the only girl I'd ever dated who insisted on keeping the lights on the first time we made love. I was afraid she'd ditch me as soon as she saw the love handles I had no trouble hiding when the guys started wearing their shirttails out.

I close the medicine book in front of me, recalling how I pulled away when she orgasmed so I could see the look on her face.

I collect the rest of my things from the table and shove them in my carry-on, moved by the fact that a rumor of death could temporarily rejoin those whom life had torn asunder. Hoisting the bag over my shoulder, I walk across the room and kiss Caroline lightly on the cheek.

Fighting back tears, Agnes cuts her eyes at the white Persian eating a lime-crusted turd from the nearby cat box. She slaps a rolled-up newspaper against the palm of her hand. "Shoo, you."

❖

Taking another sip of my fifteen-dollar chardonnay in the tiki bar near Gate 57, I leave my nose in the glass two seconds longer to avoid the ammonia scent coming from the men's room. "Crap. I forgot my toothbrush."

"I'm sure your mother will have an extra. I mean, don't all Southern mothers have an extra *everything*?"

I nod, certain Caroline's right. She's never met my mother, nor anyone else in my family. Probably because that would make it too official. "So. Gary dropped me from his roster. I'm no longer a Forefront client."

"Oh God, Phillip, no."

It took me ages to figure out the reason for my breakup with Caroline was I stayed too angry and depressed from enduring one career setback after another. I'm sure I dropped this Gary bomb as a reminder, in case she'd forgotten the ceaseless keg of nails I'd already pounded into the lid of our relationship coffin.

"This will be the final boarding call for Flight 193 to Atlanta."

"Final? I never heard the first one," I say, standing and taking one last swig from the plastic glass, cringing as I remember there are no such things as nonstops to Mobile. The joke back home is that even when you go to heaven, you still have to change planes in Atlanta. I absentmindedly attempt to figure out how to pull up the handle on the carry-on I've had for eons.

"Here, let me." Caroline kneels next to me and studies the bag, another selfless gesture from someone trying their best to say and do all the right things at a time when everything in my universe, once again, feels as if it's teetering on calamity.

"I'll carry it," I say with a grunt, balancing it in front of me like I'm moving furniture. "I mean, it's a carry-on, right?"

Caroline looks at me for a moment and kisses me on the cheek. "You be careful back there. It's all gonna—" She stops for a second. "You know, I thought about stowing away in your knapsack on your flight to Tennessee Williams–land."

"That's sweet," I say. "You're sweet." I put the suitcase down and bury my head in her bosom like a youngster panicked on the first day of school. Caroline-with-the-long-"i" pats my back like she's soothing a colicky baby. "I remember the time when I wanted to *live* right here," I moan. She lets me be for a few seconds before she pulls away and points me toward the gate.

I step out of the tiki bar and merge onto the busy concourse below. Looking over my shoulder, I see her wiping away a tear with the sleeve of her UCLA sweatshirt. I pretend I don't see it. Instead, I try to lighten the mood by fastening an imaginary noose above my head, my face bulging in comic desperation as I make my way backward to my tenuous future.

Briefly colliding with a bustling flight attendant, I straighten up, looking for one last reassuring glimpse from Caroline, but she's already gone.

The speaker above my head crackles to life. "This is the final call."

2

I come from a county on the Gulf Coast of Alabama bordering the Florida panhandle. Winston Gant, the pugnacious attorney who sold my father the lot on which he built our first house, claimed to sleep with his head in the Heart of Dixie and his butt in the Sunshine State, a report no one felt compelled to disprove.

Brewton was a colony of middle- to upper-middle-class homes built on Murder Creek, a tributary of the Conecuh River. The place got its name from a tale about a party of Royalists traveling in the 1700s from South Carolina to Pensacola who were savagely slaughtered by a roaming band of traders. Centuries later, the football teams of Brewton's T.R. Miller High School and East Brewton's W.S. Neal face off each October in a bloody combat that makes that fracas pale in comparison.

In the 1960s and 70s, the town claimed to have more millionaires than any other Southern town of its size, a fact proven by the still-standing mansions built by the early lumber barons, many of them occupied by their descendants. That tidbit, combined with the cold hard-ish fact that the area, known as the blueberry capital of the south, had also been declared one of the one hundred best small towns in America by some Yankee journalist, lent its citizens the impression they weren't adrift in a sea of paucity and ignorance.

In any case, we had all been informed at a very early age we should be damned grateful we lived in Alabama. After all, it could be much worse. We could live in Mississippi, a place I passed through twice growing up without ever finding out what made it worse than the state we already lived in.

Some idiot once said God never gives you any more than you can handle, but the way I always saw it, all you have to do is glance in any graveyard, back alley bar, or skid row refrigerator box to find those who got just that.

Tina Kimbrough, a Baptist preacher's daughter, was a product of the fifties. Homecoming queen two years in a row, she married my father, Garrett Stalworth, her high school sweetheart. Abandoning her dreams of becoming an art teacher so she could raise a family, Tina suffered three nervous breakdowns because she couldn't speak up for herself.

My father, on the other hand, chose pharmaceuticals as his profession, adjusted his blinders, and took off running. Tina developed a lifelong tell—a shallow clearing of her throat every time one of her requests to my father to take the garbage out, let the dog in, or lower the volume on the TV was ignored. "Aheeem," she'd say, completing the task herself without another word.

"Did you want something, baby?" Garrett would yell from another part of the house five minutes later.

"No," my mother would whisper, slamming the screen door, shoving a chair roughly under the table, or clanging a glass noisily in the dish drain.

When Tina was in labor with my sister, both of them almost died. The doctors forbade her to have another, instructions my mother thankfully took to heart for only a short time. According to most accounts, Sis came out of the womb bawling like a burn victim and offered those around her no relief in sight for years.

My great-aunt Violet told my mother to let her cry, advice she had gleaned from an article in *Ladies Home Journal*. But day after day, a naïvely hopeful Tina would dress Sis up in her frilly pink finest, pretending this time would be different. And day after day, the ladies of the town would nod nervously as mother and child approached, Tina offering them another opportunity to peep into the inviting confines of the carriage before they were forced to excuse themselves over another one of Sis's bloodcurdling bawls.

Aunt Violet used to tell Tina there was only so much shit a person could take before they took the reins of their life into their own hands. And although Violet drank herself to an early death because God had given her more than *she* could handle, I probably owe my life to that gin-soaked observation.

"You've got another one yet," she told my mother as they sat on opposite ends of the Formica table in our little white house on Dawson Street.

"But the doctors—"

Violet patted Tina's hand. "You've got a boy. Worth the trouble. Not like this first one. Easy labor. A happy, grateful child."

Aunt Violet was gifted with two uncanny abilities: telling the future and removing a person's wart by rubbing it with her thumbs, an art that had its roots in our ancestors' native Germany and perfected in backwoods Appalachia. Sometimes she even read the subject's fortune through the designs on the wart. On this particular day, she was removing a callus from the bottom of one of Tina's aching feet.

While Tina sipped her tea, she calmly took in her aunt's old world divination, ignoring Sis's fiery screams from the nursery upstairs.

"You should get someone to help with the other," Aunt Violet said, tilting her head in the direction of Sis's cries. She stepped on the lid release of the trash can before dropping the remains of the callus on an empty bag of English peas.

❖

When my sister was three and a half, Tina had reached the end of her rope. Returning to the car in tears from yet another humiliating scene in the A&P, when she had actually been asked to remove Sis from the premises, Tina saw an ad for Dewey's Sweet & Soft Laundry Detergent playing on ten identical televisions in the storefront window of Horton's TV & Hi-Fi. In the ad, the stunning, happy mother held her giddy, handsome baby boy playfully above her head in soft, loving focus. Stuffing a still-sobbing Sis into the back seat of the Falcon, Tina's focus drifted back to the carefree scene of mother and son before her.

I swam out—like a fish—nine months later, arriving on the heels of a storm that stole springtime blooms from gardens as far north as Birmingham. For the first time in history, the Azalea Trail, a pageant where debutants paraded in hoop skirt regalia by antebellum homes like the Civil War had only been a tale told to bad children, had to be called off.

The delivery nurse said it was the easiest birth she'd ever attended.

3

My father's father, Harold Stalworth, was a hard, quiet man who withheld his affections from a needy brood starving for it. The son of a blind tombstone salesman and a homemaker from the tiny town of Whatley, Alabama, he was a self-made success by age thirty with his own general store and taxi service. On Sunday afternoons, Poppy, as we called him, would greet me with a firm handshake, never a hug, even when I was small.

I could never reconcile the old silent figure dressed in a suit and tie in August heat with the man some said had run liquor during Prohibition just for the fun of it. The authorities could never catch him, as he tied pine limbs to the bumper of his Hudson to cover his tracks on the dirt roads of Clarke County.

Mama Louella had no nurturing traits either, having considered jumping out of a crabapple tree in order to terminate another unwanted pregnancy. The child of poor dirt farmers in northwest Florida, she wanted nothing more than to spend her days gallivanting with her younger siblings, especially since she now had a household staff to take care of the cooking and cleaning.

Decades later, Mama Louella would be watching the Pride parade coverage on the news at my Aunt Sarah's in Atlanta. "I think I could have been one o' them in a different time," she said, pointing to a militant lesbian leading the brigade.

My father's saving grace came in the form of Poppy's mother, Pauline, who practically adopted him. Realizing the existence Garrett had narrowly escaped, Pauline spent every spare second with her grandson, showering him with love and attention. An avid nature lover, she taught him everything he needed to know about the world in the piney woods around Whatley. It's because of her, and my father, that I can identify a particular species of bird, tree, or fish and tell you when it roosts, seeds, or spawns. It's a gift I wouldn't appreciate for years to come.

My aunt Sarah came across an old photo of Garrett and my uncle Thomas when they were boys, standing outside Poppy's store. Covered in dirt and meanness, they look like they'd just beaten the life out of each other. Pauline couldn't have entered at a better time.

Maybe because she made Garrett the star of the show, he was already in the habit of putting himself first by the time he came to us. Of course, it could have also just been a sign of the times. Did other men put their wives first in the fifties, sixties and seventies? I think not. I just imagine some wives handled it better than others.

Garrett was never mean, nor was he violent. In fact, he was the direct opposite. He cried every time Judy sang "Somewhere Over the Rainbow" during the annual showings of *The Wizard of Oz.* He'd tell you he loved you several times a day. Every time he walked past Sis, he'd wink and say, "Daddy's baby girl." He'd come into my dark bedroom each night to tousle my hair. If I was still awake, I'd hear him make a tiny grunt, as if to say to himself, "I made this." And much to my chagrin, he and Tina were very affectionate with each other. When he walked in after a day's work, they would share a passionate kiss before he spanked her once hard on the butt. She would giggle, and that would be that.

The thing was, the man had no interest whatsoever in our interests. We all had our obsessions. Tina had her art, Sis her music, and me movies. Garrett had work, hunting, and fishing. As far as he was concerned, never the twain shall meet. He refused to give up hope, though, that we'd come around to his way of living. He would often bore us with stories of this wife or that who loved to hunt, and kids who lived to rise at dawn to catch a fish.

I still cannot fathom just how hard I tried to love it.

One of my earliest memories is of my father and me fishing with a couple of cane poles on Porter's Lake, which lay below a rusty fence behind the backyards of the Colonial homes on Dawson Street. There wasn't a whole lot to catch in the tiny tarn except a few perch and some bluegill here and there, but it was one of the few things the two of us did together. One particular day I unexpectedly tied into a bed of shellcracker, and I yanked them in one after another, until I couldn't yank anymore. My father called me Kingfish around his friends for a year after that, beaming with pride every time he regaled them with the memory of the surprise booty.

The sunken locale of Porter's allowed voices from neighboring homes to carry across its muddy banks like a basin-shaped transistor. Those long dead could have still heard the voice of Raymond Simpkins, the six-year-old who lived three doors down, bouncing across the stagnant lake and ricocheting off the cedars below us. Raymond sang "Found a Peanut" twice as loud as anyone needed to. And always, it seemed, in the direction of my backyard.

As popular as that ditty was when I was a toddler, no one in my family was allowed to sing it anywhere near me. I am told I would fly into a blind, seething rage at the mere sound of the first few bars. The whole thing hit a bit close to home since I'd had a morbid fear of death as a young child. Raymond's woeful tune was overwhelmingly distressing: the fact that a body could be walking around, feeling fine and—just like that—something as benign as a suspect legume could snatch you willy-nilly into the next world.

When I was four, Pauline, at age eighty-two, decided to declare her independence from my rigid great-grandfather by learning how to drive. As we all gathered for a Fourth of July dinner at Aunt Sheila's on the Alabama River, news arrived that, upon returning to her house from a meeting of the DAR, Pauline had neglected to take her brand-new Oldsmobile out of gear. While making her way down the steep driveway to her front porch, the car rolled over her, taking her life and her independence just like that. Before she expired, as proof that she'd made *some* sort of a dent in this existence, she wrote her name in the sand and followed it with a big, fat period: "PAULINE CLAIRE STALWORTH."

Early on, my father had instilled in me the philosophy that if you make a decision, devise a plan, follow instructions, and carry through on all points, the universe will be more than happy to lend you a helping hand. And had my great-grandmother listened to Aunt Sheila's careful driving tips, read the owner's manual as advised, and kept an air of calm and stability about her, we would have all sat down to a nice holiday meal of fried chicken and watermelon while watching the boats leaving the dock for their holiday adventures instead of calling Luther Gaynes's ambulance service and telling him to take his time about it.

It's a lesson this control freak would never forget.

4

My practice of calling my mother and father by their first names began with a TV show. One night we were watching the first episode of the Cloris Leachman series *Phyllis*, and her strong-willed daughter referred to her mother as Phyl. I decided then and there I'd do the same and never looked back. Tina never batted an eye, but Garrett would occasionally ask, "What about just Daddy, son?" I soon learned to obliged his request whenever I wanted something. Sis followed suit, making damned sure I wasn't the only one allowed some show of disrespect.

Tina and I spent our afternoons painting still lifes in the sunroom. That is, until Sis came home from school in her usual state of provocation, and the rest of the day would go to hell in a wailing, weeping handbasket. But in those hours awaiting Sis's return, I sat patiently as my mother went over the elements of perspective, color, and horizon lines. When Tina was teaching, she was alive—a woman with purpose, a role to fulfill. But even at that age, I knew our times together couldn't fill the void she carried.

"Don't it look lonesome outside?" Tina would ask, although it seemed she was asking no one in particular as she stared out the big bay window. A straight line of water oaks dotted the far shore of the lake, barren from another Gulf Coast winter.

"I guess so," I'd say, waiting for her to chase away her usual momentary lapse into hopelessness with a more cheerful thought, the way she always did.

"There's a teaching job down at the high school," she said. "They need an art teacher for the older kids. Annie Stokes is retiring."

Annie Stokes had been the art instructor for a hundred and thirteen years and had played the organ drunk at the Church of Christ for ninety of 'em.

"You'd be good at that."

"You're darn right I would be," she answered, chewing the end of her paintbrush. "Your father thinks I should stay home."

"Oh." I already knew to stay as far away from that one as possible.

"He's probably right." She sighed, leaned over my shoulder, placed her hand over mine, and waved my pencil over the outline of apples and pears. The sad, hapless fruit bowl soon began to take on some drastically enviable dimension. "There," she said, like some contented enchantress. "You're a genius."

"Thanks," I said, brushing the charcoal off my hands, marveling at the miraculous shift of mood in the room.

"You're welcome," Tina said, glancing back at the drawing with a smile before shifting her focus once again to the lake beyond the trees.

❖

Tina had her first breakdown when I was six and a half. Her crises, big or small, invariably came during the month of April, when the blossoming world of the outdoors screamed with possibilities. Her episodes always began on an emotional high, when everything was finally going her way. This usually involved the pursuit and/or attainment of a job working outside the home.

As spring was the season for colossal church revivals, she would allow herself to be sucked into a daily dose of old-timey worship. Her evenings were spent confessing an endless litany of egocentric transgressions while praying desperately for forgiveness. This lethal cocktail of assertion and self-flagellation was a recipe for disaster.

The first time Tina got sick, we watched helplessly as she endured several weeks of sleeplessness and became increasingly agitated. We all respected her wish for silence when she returned each evening from revival. Many nights, she would disappear into the bedroom to peruse her books, refusing to cook our breakfast the following morning, sleeping most days until we came home in the afternoons.

Sitting on the pew as my family took in the final sermon of the revival, I was both captivated and terrified by the visiting evangelist, a converted Orthodox Jew by the name of Abram Appleman. With his dashing good looks and thick Russian accent, he whipped the congregation into a frenzy, which I'd never seen, since we were Baptists, not Pentecostals. The women fanned themselves sensually with the evangelist's every "thou shalt not" and "lest ye be" like they were in the presence of a movie idol. We children trembled at the disturbing visuals of heaven and hell and the menfolk amened like St. Peter was taking names.

Never one for theatricalities when it came to politics or religion, my father slept soundly against the edge of the pew. At the closing invitational, my mother whispered tearfully for Sis and me to remove our shoes like she had, saying, "We're on *holy* ground now."

Taking us by the hand, she led us what seemed like three interminable miles to the altar below the pulpit. The handsome holy roller knelt next to her, his hands on her head, whispering over her like a parent soothing a fretting child. Glancing back at my father, I imagined when he finally awakened, he would be greeted by a brand-new wife, a companion free from agitation and regret since having her woes sucked out the top of her head by the anointed foreigner.

But the following week told a different story. Tina became

weak and disoriented and refused to eat. Dr. Easelle, the family physician, recommended she be committed to an upscale mental health facility in Pensacola called Tranquilaire. I watched from my bedroom window as my father and the doctor strong-armed my mother, flailing and screaming, from the tire swing in the backyard. The waiting Buick Wildcat had pulled into the other side of the carport so as not to alert the neighbors. I shut my eyes tight as a wailing Tina socked the doctor in the jaw. She kicked at the open car door, one of her bedroom slippers flying into the boxwoods. "I'M *NOT* CRAZY!" she cried. "FILTHY LIARS!!"

I heard somebody else get socked before I turned away from the window.

❖

We were told Tina would be unable to speak to any family members, including my father, for at least a week. This left each of us to draw our own conclusions. I knew from watching movies of the week that when drug addicts went away for treatment, their loved ones were told the same thing. But this, I thought, would be different.

"Your mama's nerves just got the best of her," Garrett told Sis and me. Like the same thing could befall any of us at any given time. As if the next time I got jumpy on the way to the dentist, we could very well end up taking a detour to Pensacola. Or if Garrett got carried away with a Braves game, he could be carted off, too.

Garrett called Tina's mother, Ma Cora, to come stay with us while Tina was in the hospital. Ma Cora was a tough cookie, an elementary school teacher and second wife of a widowed Baptist minister who died before I was born. I always wondered how the two of them got together, as any pictures I'd seen of the Reverend Kimbrough suggested an old, thin, sweet-souled man who would snap like a twig if manhandled too roughly by his wife.

After my parents were married, if a week went by without

a visit from Tina, Ma Cora would call and ask her, "So, what have you been up to?" And Tina would offer a detailed account of the sick kids, school starting, church functions, or whatever trials had kept her from driving over. Ma Cora would always answer with a high-pitched, disbelieving, "Um-*HUH*!" The guilt appeared as a red flush on Tina's cheeks, and she would grab the car keys and head out the door, off to make it all right again with her iron-fisted mother.

It would be years before I would understand the degree of Ma Cora's cruelty.

❖

"I heard about your mother," Mark Powell called after me on my walk home from school. Mark was three years ahead of me and already smoked Pall Malls he took from an open carton his father carried on the dashboard of his truck.

"It's none of your business," I said, without turning around.

"Same thing happened to mine."

I kept walking but kept quiet in hopes he'd keep talking.

"Spent two months in Searcy. Two different times. They had to shock her with electricity until she finally calmed down."

Even at this age, I knew about Searcy, a creepy state hospital for the mentally ill over an hour away. Searcy was located at the end of a road off Highway 43 near McIntosh. Whenever we passed it on a road trip, Sis would nudge me and say, "This is where we drop you off."

Against my better judgment, I stopped and turned around.

"Don't let 'em do that to your mother." Mark stopped, too, waiting for a response.

"They wouldn't do that," I said with conviction.

"What makes you so sure?"

"I gotta go," I said, and walked briskly across Bellville Avenue traffic.

"Don't let 'em," he called out as I broke out into a slow trot.

I didn't even bother to retrieve the notebook I'd dropped in the street.

❖

On the first day my mother was allowed to leave Tranquilaire for the afternoon, my father took her to the Cordova Cinema to see Robert Altman's *M*A*S*H*. The poster touted something sexy, with a peace sign perched on a woman's naked legs in high heels. But even I knew the film was a poor choice. My mother detested blood and guts of any kind. She even got weak kneed the time or two she'd watched *Marcus Welby, MD* with Ma Cora, a show my grandmother never missed.

Garrett came home from his trip morose and dejected. Ma Cora, Sis, and I were seated on the sofa, waiting for a report. Garrett reclined in his La-Z-Boy. "She cried soon after the thing started until she finally said she couldn't take it anymore. She wanted to go back to the hospital, so I took her." He looked at us for some kind of salvation. Tears were streaming down his face. "And here I am."

I crawled up in his lap like I was still three. "Okay, Bo Skeet," he whimpered. "It'll be okay."

"Will they shock her, do you think?" I said.

"What do you mean?" Garrett sniffed.

"Mark Powell said they shocked his mother twice, with electricity."

"No." Garrett grabbed my hand and looked in my eyes, making sure I knew he was serious. "Your mama's at a nice place. They don't do that. Alma Powell got what she could afford. Do you understand me?"

Sis came around the other side of the recliner and laid her head in Garrett's lap. Ma Cora got up and quietly went to her room. The three of us stayed there without one more word until it was dark.

Going down the hallway for bed that night, I saw Ma Cora

crying facedown on her bed in the guest room. "My baby," I heard her say as Sis came out of the bathroom and joined me in the hall. Seeing my grandmother in such a vulnerable state was another shock to my young system. Sis went in Ma Cora's room, and I went on to bed.

"Hanner," I heard her say, "what are we gonna do?" Ma Cora had a habit of putting an "r" on the end of words ending with "a." Pulling the covers over me in my bunk bed, I could still hear her wailing in Sis's arms. "She was my baby," she cried, like Tina was already dead.

❖

Tina came home two weeks later. Like a captured animal released into the wild, she spent her days uneasily, like one of those people in the body-snatching movies. It was Tina, but it wasn't my mother. Garrett explained it was the medication she was on.

She gradually became more affectionate with us, and when we were out of school for the summer, we all began to get back into our routine of swimming, berry picking, and tennis.

Most weekdays after school, Marcie Autman, a friend from next door, came over to watch *Dark Shadows*. On one particular day, she took my attention away from werewolves and vampires with a poke in the side. She pointed incredulously to the kitchen, where my mother and father were kissing. I rolled my eyes, shrugged, and turned back to the television, pretending what I had seen was no big deal. I heard my father spank my mother once on the butt. And then I heard her giggle.

We were safe.

5

My father's voice whispers close, like temptation telling me to do something I knew I shouldn't. "Don't shoot until his head's in your sight, Bo Skeet."

The turkey gobbler fans its tail feathers near two curious hens just this side of the rusty wire fence separating my grandfather's piney woods from the state game reserve. Garrett was a hunter who followed rules and regulations to the letter. Had the wild bird chosen to preen six feet in the other direction, the odds of its living out the day would have increased exponentially. Even so, a nine-year-old with no kills on record shouldn't have given the creature any cause for concern.

"Now, don't *pull* the trigger, Bo Skeet, *squeeeeze* it gently. *Eeeasy* does it." I can hear his heart beating louder than mine.

The gobbler retracts its feathers, drums a sound of concern, and stops cold. It looks just like a picture on a place mat I'd seen at a log cabin restaurant on summer vacation in Tennessee.

I feel Garrett nod stealthily, and I squeeze the trigger at the same exact time the shotgun kicks me in the shoulder, knocking me into his arms. The earth-shattering report camouflages the sounds any survivors would have made in retreat.

"Thataway!" Garrett shouts. "That's Daddy's boy!" He pulls me close into the fold of his big brawny arms. "I didn't believe you could do it," he says, cackling, jostling me like an oversized baby. "I swear to the good Lord, I didn't believe you could do it!"

The hens are nowhere in sight. I step over the bright red shotgun shell as I walk over to the fence where the gobbler had been thrown, one of its brightly colored wings flung like a cape over what once was its head.

"I thought he was gone. I saw the sonofabitch flap his wings once. I says, 'That's it, he's gone.' But he wasn't," my father crows, patting me on the back, squatting to give me another hug. "Daddy's boy," he says again as he picks up the kill by a withered foot.

I smell blood as I reach out to touch one of the gobbler's wings. I take the bird by its other foot, surprised at the weight of the warm, lifeless thing, and gallantly throw the shotgun over my shoulder as the congratulatory whoops of the other hunters ricochet over the hill.

The golden brown leg stares back at me from my Easter dinner plate between the mashed potatoes and green bean casserole. The sad, crispy carcass radiates a noxious aura of compunction and shame. I never knew becoming the son my father always wanted would feel so rotten.

"Something wrong with your dinner, son?" my mother asks timidly from across the dining room table. Her face is partially hidden by a carnival-style tumbler made specifically for Southerners and their unquenchable thirst for iced tea.

I attempt to avoid my father's gawp, his eyes glued to the remains in front of me, a sliver of bright, white breast meat crusted to the side of his mouth. "Everything okay, Bo Skeet?"

"It's fine." My eyes connect briefly with Tina's before I drag a fried onion through its cream of mushroom pottage.

"Oh my goodness, I almost forgot," Tina says. She grabs my plate and hers and disappears quickly into the kitchen.

"What'd you forget, punkin'?" Garrett says, reaching for the pitcher of tea.

"Just—oh…" I can tell Tina is stalling. The tinkling of glass and jars signal an impromptu symphony of cunning and desperation. "Two seconds," she says, as Sis sucks the life from the other drumstick, watching me like I'm the rinky-dink intermission act in a two-bit circus. Garrett carves another slab from the cadaver and plops it on his plate, his eyes never leaving mine. It was a pitiful look. A look that said he was going to lose this one.

"Ohhhhhkeydokey…" Just before enough time passes for the whole thing to go straight to hell, Tina reappears at the table with our plates. "I swear, sometimes I think I'd forget my head if it wasn't screwed on." Bending like a waiter in a four-star eatery, she returns my plate and her own. Something tells me whatever she's doing is a feeble attempt to make this whole thing go down easier, both figuratively and literally.

"The heck," Garrett says, eyeballing my drumstick and Tina's slice of meat, both now slathered in deep red, runny gravy.

"It's the sauce. For the turkey," Tina says, holding out her hands for Garrett's and Sis's plates. "It's Eye-talian."

"Nuh-uh," Sis grunts, pulling her plate in close with both arms.

"Turkey doesn't need any sauce far's I'm concerned," Garrett says, still squinting at my plate.

"Fine," Tina says, unfazed. She takes her seat and drops her napkin into her lap.

"What's it made of?" I say gingerly, wondering if the cure is worse than the ill.

"Oh, let's see, it's got ketchup, Worcestershire, and, well, let's see—Heinz 57, pure grape jelly. All your favorite things," she says, setting the bowl on the table.

Sis makes a face. "It's cold?"

"They do it all the time in It'ly," Tina says.

"Land sakes." Garrett sniffs at it.

I take a judicious bite before realizing that, solely for my benefit, Tina has whipped up something really good.

Garrett dabs a thumb into the concoction on my plate and licks it curiously. "Hmm," he says. Lifting the boat over his plate, he spoons out the rest. "Hm," he says again, grabbing a piece of turkey breast with his fingers, running it through the sauce, and popping it in his mouth. "Good stuff, doll," he says out the side of his mouth, cutting his eyes once more at me, "but it would have been fine without it."

❖

The following April, Garrett began having problems with his lower back. The issue started as an occasional spasm, prompting him to leave work early. A couple of hours on the sofa with the heating pad usually did the trick. Sis and I would remain uncharacteristically quiet and let him choose whatever he wanted to watch on TV. By early evening, he'd get up and hobble around the house until he was back to his old self.

Just after school one day, I spot the ambulance parked in our driveway as I round the corner in front of the Gordons' place. When I race in the carport door, my father is flat on his back by the fireplace. My mother and sister are hugging the sides of the sofa, the paramedics crouched over him.

"I can't get up, Bo Skeet."

"We're gonna take your dad to the hospital," one of the paramedics says.

"Can I ride with him?"

"You stay here with your Sis," Tina says, standing.

I take Garrett's hand.

"It's the craziest thing, son. I can't move."

"He'll be okay," the other paramedic says. Garrett shrieks in pain as they lift him on the stretcher.

The look on Tina's face says it hurts her more than it does him.

"I'm going with your father," she says to us. "Ma Cora should be here within the hour."

Two days later, Garrett was released from the hospital. After a battery of tests, the doctors were at a loss. "Could have been a pulled muscle, a pinched nerve, or just plain stress," Dr. Lowell said.

After several weeks of recuperation, Garrett never suffered from back pain again. I often wondered if my father had worked himself into a twisted, tortured mess with the approach of another spring, when his wife could wind up who knows where. However it happened, the events of that April did, in fact, take the focus off my mother. During a time of year when she would find herself most vulnerable, she put all her energy into helping Garrett get well. In the process, she felt needed.

The rest of the spring and summer passed without incident.

6

Scrubbing the last crunchy love bug of the autumn season off the Wildcat's windshield, I check the rest of the humongous car's windows for smudges. For years now, it's been my duty to keep the shine on my father's cars in tip-top shape.

"Stalworth. You're gonna take the paint off if you scrub any harder," my eleven-year-old friend Greggie calls quietly from a patch of darkness in the far corner of the utility room.

I spit one last time across one of Sis's grimy paw prints on the passenger's side. Garrett loved his big cars. And this one was the biggest ever.

Greggie accidentally knocks something over and makes his way out of the shadows and into my sweaty field of vision just inside the garage door. "Hey."

Wiping my forehead with the chamois, I peer over the open car door at a grinning Greggie making his way tentatively into the light, the waist of his Wranglers around his knees, his erect penis jumping like the ruby throat of a chameleon sunning itself on a lakeshore stump.

"What the hell are you *doing*?"

Greggie shrugs, taking another step into the late afternoon sun.

"Whoa," I say, tossing the chamois over my shoulder. Thinking he must be in the throes of some meltdown brought on by his sorry-assed mother's escalating whiskey intake, I jump out of the car and race toward him. Greggie pulls the foreskin over the glans of his organ and stretches it out as far as it will go, looking dead into my eyes with a raised brow, like he just pulled a rabbit out of a hat. "At least get away from the door," I say, yanking him into the corner.

Greggie pulls at the zipper of my khakis. "Show me yours."

I push his hand away. "I can't. Wait." Greggie is laughing and, oddly enough, so am I.

"What the Sam Hill's going on out here, boys?" Garrett stands in the open doorway of the utility room, arms crossed across his chest like a comic book genie.

"Shit," Greggie says, zipping up.

I make a sorry attempt to drop my hands nonchalantly in front of my own open zipper.

Garrett surveys the scene in silence. He finally straightens a bass net hanging haphazardly from a wooden peg on the wall next to him without looking at us. "Greggie, I think you need to get on home now."

Greggie scoots swiftly past my father, offering up a hoarse "Yessir" over his shoulder before disappearing out the door.

I absentmindedly take the chamois off my shoulder and wipe my hands, shifting from one foot to the other. "I—"

"Make it spotless, Bo Skeet," Garrett says, heading out, glancing once over his shoulder with a familiar look of disappointment.

Several minutes pass before I can pick up the chamois again. Standing in the same place, I wonder if Garrett could tell just how engrossed I was in the goings-on with Greggie. I replay the scene over in my head like a television sports announcer. After all, I thought, he had walked in at the moment when my focus had gone from confusion to excitement. I pray he missed the shift.

I kept going back to the business with Greggie, attempting to block my father out of the scene. However fleeting, the experience was like none other I'd ever had. Of course, I'd peed in the woods with other male friends. One would try and take the other by surprise and spray his shoe, but this felt like all that times twenty. Although I wished Greggie and I had been able to explore a bit more, I knew it would never happen again. We'd both been humiliated during a defenseless moment. Who would ever want to revisit that?

I grabbed the chamois and went back to work. I was determined to make this the cleanest the car had ever been.

❖

Tina spreads another brand-new *Batman* across the bottom bunk. The bounty we'd scored from a three-hour comic-buying trip was meant to lift my spirits from the cold hard fact that we were leaving the only life we'd ever known behind. The idea that I was the cause of Garrett's decision to uproot the whole family made this new reality unbearable. I still wasn't aware if he'd told Tina what had transpired two weeks ago in the utility room with Greggie. And if he had, would that alone send her off for another stint at Tranquilaire?

"Now, what in the world could you have done to make you think that we're moving because of you?" Tina says, stacking the magazines in a neat pile on the bedside table. "Did something happen?"

I keep mum, satisfied she was in the dark. "Listen," she says, sitting on the bed, pulling me down next to her. "Here's a news flash. Whenever your father makes a decision, it doesn't involve anybody else but him, you understand? And this is a big promotion. He'll have his own office instead of being out in the field, which is a good thing. And it's only an hour away, so you can still see Greggie and Marcie and whoever else whenever you want."

"Well, why doesn't he just drive? It's not that far. I mean, Farley West's daddy works nearly all the way to Point Clear, and he drives it every day."

Tina gives me my answer by turning her mouth into a straight line.

"But it's Redneck Ridge," I say, referring to the moniker Brewton's football team had tagged the town of Jackson with on our trips to play them.

"I'll admit, it's not as culturally rich as Brewton. I mean, there's no college like we have here and that makes a difference. But it's on the river. Do you know how much fun you can have on the river? Not a puny backyard puddle like you're used to here. And your father's decided you'll be going to the Academy. That's a terrific opportunity."

"The Academy?" I say, horrified. "That's a military school!"

Tina laughs. "Where in the world did you get that idea? Lord, your father decides to move his entire family because of you, and then he decides to punish you by putting you in military school? Sounds like something Faulkner would have come up with. The Academy is *not* a military school and you well know it," she says. "It's just a private school. With better teachers and just—better everything."

I knew better. From what Tom Grant, a recent transfer from the Academy told me, the entire basis of existence for the brand-new school was to keep the more affluent white kids from having to learn next to the black kids, a belated way to spit in the face of desegregation without having to come out and say it. Tom Grant knew what he was talking about. Sleek, single-story schools were popping up all over the South like toadstools after a hard, soggy rain. According to reports, the Academy was proving to be one of the most poorly administrated, with a lack of any sports or activities beyond football and honors clubs.

"Your uncle Donald knows the headmaster. He wants to take you over there this afternoon, and they're gonna show you around."

"*This* afternoon?"

Tina stares at her hands in her lap, her fingers toying with her wedding band. "Bo Skeet," she says, "truth be told, I'm wrestling with this one, too. But I don't know what to say to make it any better." Tina grabs one of the springs underneath the upper bunk and pulls. "I know this sounds crazy, but sometimes I'll pretend I'm someone else until whatever unpleasantness passes." She looks at me, almost embarrassed. "You know, I'll be whoever I want to—Mama Louella, Lurleen Wallace," she says, flashing a brief, reckless smile. "Even *Jane Fonda*, woo-hoo."

Through the window, I see Garrett wiping off the radio antenna of the Wildcat, a task I'd seen him do many times when preparing for a trip or excursion he was enthusiastic to begin. Glancing back at one of the comic books, I'm thinking Robin and I could take care of the whole business with a series of *ZONKs* and *POWs*.

Tina clears her throat. "You'll make new friends, and you'll learn so much. You'll see. In no time at all, you'll be thanking your father." She spits in her hand and smooths my hair, the only person outside of the movies I'd ever known to spit on anything in hopes of making it better.

Later, when my father steers the Wildcat slowly onto Dawson Street, I can hear Tina slam the front door of the house four times *hard* before she goes inside.

7

Shortly after we moved to Jackson, Aunt Violet told Garrett he could either find Tina a good housekeeper or a good divorce lawyer.

Fanny came to us through a friend who had to let her go when they moved out of state. A tiny, deeply religious person who looked like Cicely Tyson, Fanny hated card playing of any kind. Sis and I were always looking for the chance to deal a hand of spades just so we could watch her leave the room like her pants were on fire. Behind her back, we lovingly referred to Fanny as Worst Case Scenario, because no matter how bad you *thought* things could get, Fanny was always there to tell you just *how* bad.

Fanny loved movies. She also loved Omar Sharif. Monday afternoons, Sis and I gathered on the back porch where Fanny treated us to the details of whatever flick she had caught over the weekend, her short, nimble fingers relieving a mess of freshly picked field peas from their tough shells with a coarse, staccato *ziiiip*. Needless to say, our hero's lowest points were punched the hardest, as were the endings, which she gave away first. "So. Zhivago and this lady are in all this snow. And theeen he dies. On the bus. After *all* that."

"So," she'd say with another *ziiiip* and a nod of her head, intimating the same fate could happen to any of us hearing the tale of horror and disappointment for the first time.

My father had recently begun visiting his brother in Grove Hill after church since we now lived closer. My mother decided those afternoons were going to belong to her. Most Sundays, she'd send me to the movies with my increasingly incensed sister. I pleaded with Tina to let me explore the creeks and gullies of Walker Springs Road with my new bucktoothed friend Billy Wade Gorman, but she said she'd rather know my exact whereabouts. Billy Wade's father owned the local cement business and insisted on carting us around in his big silver cement truck, a vehicle which made Tina nervous. If I was with Sis, she wouldn't have to worry.

Sis had decided to hold me personally responsible for Tina's uncharitable act with a set of stringent ground rules that changed from week to week.

"I swear to God, if you act for *one split second* like you know me I will scratch your face off, do you understand me?"

Easy so far.

"You are to *quietly* and *calmly* approach me at intermission to see if I want anything. And if I do, you'll take it out of *your* allowance."

Okay. So this was gonna hurt.

"Aaand if I ever *get* to the theatre and find I've forgotten something—chewing gum or compact, *whatever*—then *you* have to go home and get it. And you can't complain. 'Cause if you do, I'll scratch your face off."

Stringent rules aside, I soon became addicted to our weekly excursions to the Locke Theatre in downtown Jackson. Its crimson seats and tiled floors were kept sparkling clean by the Baileys, a Yankee couple in their seventies who had a checklist as rigid as my sister's. Tiny as a stick with hair dyed just as brittle, Mrs. Bailey ran the box office with a clipped dialect that made her sound like she was from a different planet.

"*One* ticket. That will be *one* fifty," she said. "One" sounded like "wan," and we all mocked her when out of earshot.

Mr. Bailey was a World War II veteran who had lost both

legs in combat, a fact that made him even more intimidating as he raced up and down the aisles at breakneck speed, his muscular hands propelling the wheels of the bright gold wheelchair, his teeth bared like a defensive James Cagney. "*No* running, *no* talking, and positively *no* fighting," he'd say.

This last admonition was strictly for the Dick brothers, three fat redneck siblings who proceeded to beat each other senseless during the opening cartoon every Sunday probably, we decided, over the shared ignominy of their unfortunate last name.

Mr. Bailey would wheel his chair to a small control booth he'd constructed behind a navy blue curtain at the rear of the auditorium. There, he'd crank the volume to fit the mood during emotional peaks of the films. Whenever we saw the glint of one of Mr. Bailey's wheels hustling up the aisle toward his beloved sound box, we knew something was gonna happen, and that something was gonna be good.

When the whistling score crescendoed, we knew the bridge over the River Kwai was gonna go. When the waves swelled so potently from the depths of the Atlantic we could actually feel it in our chests, there was no question the *Poseidon*'s seconds were numbered. Mrs. Haney, my fifth-grade teacher, said *Love Story* wouldn't have been half as sad if Mr. Bailey had left well enough alone.

When the music pumped to ten decibels during Scarlett's dirty radish scene in *Gone With the Wind*, Beulah Money, the librarian at the Methodist church, marched right up to Mr. Bailey and demanded he turn the blasted thing down, adding, "Those same bombs that took your legs in France must have snatched what was left of your hearing along with it."

One of the drawbacks to Sunday matinees was that musicals always started on Sundays and played through Tuesdays, and I'd had to sit through more than my share. Sis liked to rub this in since musicals were her favorite and she knew I didn't feel the same. I saw them all: *Chitty Chitty Bang Bang, The Sound of Music, Paint Your Wagon,* and every period piece Barbra Streisand warbled her way through.

One particular Sunday, having offered Sis a whole dollar to let me off the hook to no avail, I found myself watching *Cabaret*, yet another musical starring no one I'd ever heard of. From what I could tell from the previews, the movie was about Nazis and drunken whores hanging out in smoky German bars.

Patience Harmon, a comely fellow fifth grader from down the street, spotted me sitting by myself in my usual seat on the front row. She offered to sit next to me, a proposal I readily accepted, since Patience had the reputation of being a bit loose herself. Patience was one of five offspring belonging to a drab, blank-faced couple who read from the Gospels in lieu of giving away candy on Halloween. Her Bible-thumping parents would have suffered joint coronaries had they known what a bowlful of junk she was being corrupted with on this particular Sunday.

At a spot far into the film, the whore and her two handsome male friends were drunk, as usual, and dancing, as usual. But this time, they were all three dancing together, and the depraved manner in which they were ogling each other told me this scene was different from anything I'd come across in those other witless Sunday trifles. A wakefulness in the pit of my stomach felt vaguely familiar, like that split second when the cork on the end of your line disappears as a perch finally takes the bait.

And then somebody started singing some kind of German drinking song. I was thinking Patience was going to say something dumb and spoil the moment, but she didn't. I worried Mr. Bailey would blast past us on his way to the sound box, but he didn't. I guess he figured he shouldn't play up the aberrant godlessness on the screen any more than was necessary.

Maybe, like me, he thought the visuals spoke for themselves.

❖

"What did you think about the end? When she found out he was screwing her *and him?*" Patience stops mid-whisper, tossing the top of her hamburger bun into the trash can next to our picnic table in front of Gill's Burger Hut. Sis had dumped us at the fly-infested rattrap so she could walk home with Randall Creighton, a handsome sophomore. Randall's father ran a funeral home in Sloan County and reeked of formaldehyde and something else no one could put their finger on.

"Yeah, I know."

"You think they were queer? Like Solomon?" Patience glances toward the open order window where a tall, skinny black man is sweating behind the griddle.

"Who knows?" I say, picking off the green, diseased tip of a French fry.

A resident of the Depot, the black community across the railroad tracks, Solomon Davidson was what I would later understand to be transgender, and not a very good one. Solomon always seemed to have thrown himself together at the last minute, with a floral print housedress gathered haphazardly about his neck, a black patent leather purse gaping open, or a scuffed pump missing a heel. No makeup, hat, or belt completed the ensemble, as if he dressed as a woman only as an afterthought.

It was probably this lack of specificity that saved him a great deal of ridicule. I'm still amazed Fat Gill Loper, a deacon at First Baptist, thought no more about hiring him than the man in the moon. And strangely enough, I can never recall someone lowering their window to yell an epithet in Solomon's direction. Even Patience, the queen of yelling shit out of car windows, never yelled anything. The worst I'd ever heard about him was a rumor that he smashed out the raw hamburger patties by slipping them under his armpit. I'd always found this hard to believe, as did Patience, since she was now on her second paper-thin burger.

"Mama says the devil took part of Solomon's mind, but I don't know," Patience says. "Mama thinks the devil took part of *everybody's* mind, prob'ly even mine."

I took another fry from the mound on the wax paper and wondered what Solomon would think about the horny trio we'd seen today. And I wondered, if he had the means, would he walk the streets of Jackson in the getups the drunken whore wore in the movie, or would he save it for his mirror at home where no one else could see?

❖

The scent of sea water and creosote floods through the open windows of the Buick Electra 225. Six months after we moved, Garrett had traded in the old Buick for an even bigger one. Sis and I are catnapping in the back seat on our return from a Stalworth family reunion in Gulf Shores. The air is cool for late spring. My parents' soft, sporadic thoughts on the day's festivities break the monotony of the *clunk clunk clunk* of the Causeway Bridge below us.

"Do you think she had any idea?" Tina says to Garrett.

"Nah."

"Do we know how long it was going on before she found out?"

"Before we found out *what*?" Sis, usually impossible to wake on a nighttime ride, sits up with a yawn and leans on the back of my father's seat.

"Y'all go back to sleep," Garrett says.

"What are we talking about?" I say. My mother has never held any family business away from her children. And it doesn't take much prodding to get her to spill.

Tina turns her head in our direction. I can see the reflection of her profile in the lights of the Bankhead Tunnel straight ahead. "Amos is leaving Janis for his golf buddy. And, yes, his golf buddy is a man."

"Tina…" Garrett acts like he's going to reprimand her again, but leaves it at that.

Sis pulls herself closer to Tina. "Are you kidding me?"

"No, I'm not kidding you. And if there's one thing you need to understand, it's that the Stalworths don't love like other people."

"Honey…" Garrett draws it out, his last protest on the subject.

Inside the well-lit tunnel, it may as well be daylight. A Mack truck gets too close for Garrett's comfort.

"Bastard," Garrett says, blowing the horn.

"The men don't just love men and the women don't just love women." Tina puts up the electric windows, an act that makes everything that follows seem even more earth-shattering. "Not your father, of course. But your great-aunt Frieda? Remember her?"

"Uh-huh," Sis says, transfixed.

I still haven't moved. I'm not sure I can.

"Caught with a minister's wife at a women's retreat."

Sis looks at me and makes an "O" with her mouth.

"Your great-grandfather Stalworth?"

I'm not sure I can stand it.

"Hoooney…"

"Took up with a piano tuner named Eddie from Pike County after Flora passed. *Aaand*," Tina says, raising a finger for effect, "he looked just like Clark Gable."

"Okay," Garrett says. "Story time's over. You young'uns get some rest. School day's gonna come mighty early."

We all disappear into the pitch black as we leave the tunnel.

Sis pinches me on the leg. Leaning back in her seat, she faces me, her mouth in the shape of another O.

I turn myself away from her and look out the window. Underneath the lights of the state docks in the distance, I picture the ancient portrait of my great-grandfather that hangs in the hallway kissing Clark Gable. I am unable to shake the visual for days.

8

Our first full summer in Jackson was in full swing. Sis stayed out of my way as she was now fourteen and consumed with boys and music. She would occasionally storm into my bedroom with a new stack of record albums. "This is James Taylor. You'll love it the first time. Joni Mitchell and David Bowie you'll hate, but keep listening to them no matter how much you hate it. And stop listening in on my phone conversations. I know it's you."

I struggled with the weekly piano lessons Tina signed me up for. Sis mastered that and everything else: trumpet, mandolin, and fiddle. I checked my ego at the door when she offered to teach me guitar with the other students she taught in the basement. She kicked me out in less than a week. "You're hopeless," she said. "In so many ways I can't even tell you."

❖

My mandatory time served at the Locke kick-started my lifelong fascination with the world of movies. I tried desperately to get Garrett to accompany me on my matinee outings, something both of us would enjoy. Much to my chagrin, he always countered with an offer to join him in some activity that would eventually lead to an animal's untimely death.

In what I considered the most egregious slap in the face of my love for cinema, Garrett would bail during the last five minutes of any movie he was forced to watch. Like clockwork, Tina, Sis, and I would strain to hear the crucial last words of a film over the *pop* of the lever on his recliner. As the plane's propeller sputtered to life on the runway behind Ilsa and Rick in *Casablanca*, Garrett stood, stretching and yawning like a bear. "I've had enough," he'd say, disappearing into the kitchen for a piece of cake.

"You can't tell me you don't give one whit as to what happens to these poor people!" Tina hollered.

"Y'all can tell me how it ends," he'd always say. But he never asked.

❖

"I'll show you mine if you show me yours," Patience says. She climbs the ladder to the roof of the tree house and sits next to me. From my perch, I can easily command the battalion of boy and girl soldiers on the ground below me through the lens of an imaginary camera.

"Patience, you're the assistant director. You're supposed to be on the ground," I bark half-heartedly.

Patience undoes the bottom two buttons of her baseball jersey and pulls out the elastic waistband of her shorts. "You better look now, 'cause now's the only chance you're gonna get."

Taking a moment to gauge whether this is a setup or some unexpected gift from the movie gods, I remember Fanny pointing out a picture of Warren Beatty in one of the *Screen Talk!* magazines she kept in her big leather purse. "Women throw themselves at this man, huh?" she'd say with a wink. Since Fanny closely followed my obsession with film, I'm sure she thought herself useful in pointing out a future problem.

Patience puts her other hand on her hip and taps her foot. I peer over the edge of the tree house, checking the activity on the ground below us. Mindy Bradford picks her nose with a grimy thumb, Tommy Grant hawks a loogie at nothing in particular, and Billy Wade casts a knowing glance up the ladder, like he's waiting for me to invite him to the party.

"TAKE FIVE, EVERYBODY!" I call with Patience's cheerleading megaphone, a vital set prop I'd doctored into a more masculine director's bullhorn with glue and covers from my father's *Field & Stream* magazines. "Billy, you're in charge of the extras!"

Billy's shoulders slump in disappointment as he slowly turns around, taking in the motley crew of misfits around him. His radically bowed horse teeth serve as a natural bullhorn of his own. "Okay, nobody move until Bo Skeet says, 'Action!'"

Thankful for the respite and anxious to get a peek at what Jimmy Quinn had already confided in me was "no big whoop," I hear the screen on the back porch door slam.

"SON, ARE YOU DRESSED WARM ENOUGH?"

Unwilling to glance in Tina's direction from this vulnerable position, I call out timidly over my shoulder. "Yes. I am."

"ARE YOU PLAYING FAIR?"

I choose not to answer this one.

"BO SKEET?"

Giggles from the troops below.

"Yes, I'm playing fair!" I say.

I hear the screen door creak open again, my mother on her way back into the house. "FOR GOD'S SAKE, RUN IN THE HOUSE IF THE SKEETER TRUCK COMES!" This last warning referenced the bug truck that drove through Gulf Coast neighborhoods late summer evenings. The rattletrap vehicle left behind clouds of foul black smoke in an effort to knock out the virulent mosquito population. Not only did it not work, the thought of inhaling the fumes terrified everyone—but none more than Tina. Jeff Jenkins, a junior high math whiz, defied these concerns by riding his bike directly behind the bug killer, inhaling deeply, laughing maniacally as everyone else ran for cover.

"Hurry," Patience says, flapping her hands at her sides.

The shadows of the lush summertime foliage above us makes for sorry sight lines. I can detect nothing but pitch black below me as Patience takes my hand and puts it down her pants. For the briefest of moments my fingers bump clumsily around in sweet, sweaty obscurity, making contact with nothing and everything at the same time.

"Is that it?"

"Shut up!" Patience says.

This time the sensation feels less like hooking a perch and more like pulling myself back from a dangerous point on a high ledge. It's a feeling I try to prolong while gently continuing my cramped exploration.

"That's it," Patience says, pushing my hand away and closing her shorts with a *snap* of elastic. "Okay, Scene 36! Let's go!" she calls over the edge of the tree house, buttoning her shirt with a grin. Patience heads down the ladder, and I'm once again the most powerful figure on the set.

THE DIXIE

May 9, 1999
Letters to the Editor

It is with no small sense of urgency that I call on my fellow brothers and sisters of Clarke County to vote with their hearts and minds next month regarding the proposed permit to allow the sale of alcohol within the city limits. This fine county of ours, since its inception, has been a beacon to those surrounding us who have chosen to recreate in inebriated revelry. Our children's future lies in the hands of those who will approach the polls with the welfare of these young, impressionable ones first and foremost on their conscience. Members of the spiritual community who wish to join our door-to-door campaign in making our citizens aware of this potentially catastrophic ordinance should join us in the fellowship hall of Fairweather Baptist Church Saturday morning at 7. Deacons will be equipping all volunteers with pamphlets on alcoholism and divorce.

Yours in The Word,
The Reverend C.C. Tompkins

9

Six hours and one Xanax-induced catnap later, I'm on my way to baggage claim as a local reporter bemoans the serious lack of rain on the Gulf Coast from a blaring TV in the terminal. A teaser for the afternoon talk shows reminds me to call Frances to inform her that her Oprah dress is ready for pickup.

"You're coming back soon, right?" Frances says, talking to at least three other people at the same time.

"As soon as I possibly can. And I'll still be handling some of the things we talked about, so don't freak out."

"Thank God. Contrary to what you may believe, I do plan on respecting your time there."

"Thanks," I say without believing a word of it. I retrieve my bags and walk outside, horrified to see Billy Wade jumping out of the cement truck he got after he inherited his daddy's concrete business. "Listen," I say to Frances, setting down my bags, shielding my eyes from the Alabama sun. "I gotta go. My ride's here."

"Call me soon. Like yesterday."

"Yup," I say, marveling at how she could make a promise in one breath and take it away in the next.

Billy Wade spits a brown stream of tobacco juice through a bucktoothed grin. Billy has held me over his head since we were kids. I mean this literally, not figuratively. Although I am of average height and weight, Billy stands well over six feet, with arms like a lumberjack. He has claimed this height since he was fifteen. Billy grabs me around the tops of my legs, hoisting me high in the air above him, running in circles until I threaten to put his eyes out with my thumbs. This warning is meant to conceal the glee in knowing most people never get to know the exhilaration of being tossed high in the air after the age of two and a half.

"How's Mr. California?" This being the first thing Billy always asks when he hasn't seen me in a while.

"Ha ha."

"Hey! I'll show you mine if you show me yours!" A bleached blonde Patience hangs off the running board of Billy's ride in blue jean cutoffs and a bikini top, late thirties be damned.

"Good God," I say as she jumps off the running board and into my arms like I was a long-lost war vet. "Look at you."

Patience laughs, flips her hair and jiggles her bosom. "Yeah, look at me," she says.

❖

Jackson, Alabama, the place we all wound up, is known as the turkey hunting capital of the universe. The town of four thousand is framed on two sides by cemeteries, the black community on the third, and on the fourth by Plymouth, the paper mill most in the town owed their livelihoods to. A behemoth with two smokestacks standing guard over the muddy Tombigbee River, Plymouth was a Yankee outfit from Idaho that initially had promised wealth and prosperity.

In the end, it failed to deliver more than a cut-rate shopping center and a Kentucky Fried Chicken. In small-town Alabama, the affluence of any town was always measured by the number of fast food chains the Chamber of Commerce landed, usually springing up on the outskirts of town so as to attract the four-lane traffic. Thomasville, half an hour away, had a Hardee's, a

McDonald's, *and* a Sonic Burger, and they didn't even have a paper mill. It was a sore subject to most in the community, and one of the most consistent bones of contention brought up at town meetings until councilman Tetley Crane forbade anyone to mention it again.

Presently, the worst drought in almost two hundred years had left the Deep South a shriveled dust bowl of end-of-the-world insanity. Dehydrated dogs died in the streets and nervous housewives shot their philandering husbands in double-wide trailers. Everywhere I look, the red dirt powder hangs in clumps from oak leaves like fake snow at Christmas.

I take my place tentatively in the back seat. Billy can't drive, and he never could. He steers the cement truck like he owns the road. Billy blows his horn at an innocent pedestrian, plowing through a traffic light that turned red five seconds ago.

"*My* side of the road!" Billy croaks. Riding shotgun, Patience hollers out the window at an old man shaking his fist as he makes his way safely to the other side of the street. "The light was still green, bonehead!"

Billy grins at Patience, who plops her bare feet on the dashboard and twists her neck around the headrest. "How's the schoolmarm?" she asks, always more concerned about the stats of one's love life than anything else.

"She's a professor, and we're sort of busted up."

She winks. "I'm just pullin' your leg, sugar. And I'm sorry about the bust-up."

"How's Granny?" I ask. Patience had years ago relocated back to Jackson to care for her favorite relative. The matriarch, a lifelong *All My Children* fan, had absentmindedly begun mingling her own milieu with that of Pine Valley.

"Granny's okay, I guess. She's positively rabid about Erica's wedding, so I was charged with the task of finding a gift for someone who's currently doing time in the hoosegow for burying someone alive."

"What about you, Billy?" I say. "How's the better half?"

Patience stage whispers, "Oh, we don't talk about that."

A spray of Billy's tobacco juice hits the window separating me from the scalding heat of an early June day in the cradle of the Gulf Coast. He pops a CD into the player on the dash. "There's a porn burglar on the loose."

"I'm sorry?" I say, the Black Eyed Peas muffling the first part of Billy's bulletin.

"Somebody's breakin' into single guys' houses with a crowbar and stealin' their porn. He's hit Griff Watson twice—some of his classic Ginger Lynn you know he'll never replace. You 'member that girl Brianne you used to date in college? Her sister's the detective on the case." Billy swerves to avoid a speeding ambulance. "*My* side of the road!"

Just ahead, a farmer hauling hay in an ancient truck approaches in the opposing lane of Highway 43. There's an old Southern superstition: if you ever meet a hay truck, you're supposed to make a wish. But it's *very* important you don't look back. Because even if you see that hay truck in your rearview mirror, your wish won't come true.

Billy pulls at a scab on his elbow, our colossal vehicle moving into the direct path of the truck.

Patience screams to me excitedly over the seat. "Hay truck, make a wish. Don't look back!"

Bowing my head, I try to think of something good to wish for. I quickly decide on wishing the events of the past few days are a figment of my imagination.

Billy whistles, swerves back into our lane and turns up Fergie. "You didn't look back, didja?"

"No," I say. "I can't believe they still do this down here."

"What'd you wish for?" Patience says.

"I think I wished that we wouldn't run into that hay truck."

"Birdie Haines saw a hay truck in her rearview mirror and *both* her babies were born dead," Patience says.

"I don't believe that."

"They were too born dead," she retorts.

"I believe *that*," I say. "I just don't think the hay truck had anything to do with it."

"Suit yourself," Billy says. "See if we care, Mr. California Know-Everything."

Patience chimes in. "Yeah, Mr. California Know-Everything."

Patience covers the rearview mirror with her hand.

Like a good Southern boy, I bow my head and close my eyes again, giving the powers that be one more chance to make all this insanity right.

10

I wave goodbye to my old friends, watching as the cement truck chugs out of sight of the big Tudor house on Blue Forest Road. Approaching the carport with my luggage, I prepare to meet head-on these dear people I see for a few days once a year. They will greet me with all the love and understanding they can muster for someone who left the small-town south for a life of smog and godlessness. They will wait on me hand and foot, call in long-lost friends and relatives, and for the time being pretend, as they always do, that their prodigal son has made a valiant life for himself.

But this time no one is here to greet me. I glance into the top of the monkey pine my grandmother Stalworth planted near the swimming pool. A hawk swirls in the edges of a cloud beyond the uppermost bough. If I were in one of the spaghetti westerns I spent time with as a boy, I'd check the water in my canteen and pray the hawk sensed something else half-dead in the area.

A brand-spanking-new ivory pickup sparkles next to my mother's five-year-old powder blue Lincoln Town Car. My father has bought a new pickup every other October as long as I can remember, as soon as the new models come out. He studies the brochures all summer long from his La-Z-Boy in the living room. He falls asleep for his afternoon nap looking at them, and they're the first thing he picks up when he pads out of the bedroom at five thirty a.m.

It's cool in the carport, and it smells like gasoline and pool chlorine. I hear a phlegmy wheeze from the adjacent storage room my father calls the Little House, its door standing ajar. A tiny sneeze from the area of the refrigerator freezer summons me closer. A mangy-looking Yorkie mix carefully creeps down the two cement steps to the carport, baring its two remaining teeth as I gingerly set down my luggage. It smells old, wet, and sour.

"No way," I say out loud. The beast moves an inch closer with a low growl, flies swarming around her oozing eyes and a dirty butt she's too old to clean.

"Here, Puffy-Puffy-Puffy!" Jewel Ann crows from her house across the road.

There's an old saying: "There's a mean dog for every Baptist south of the Mason-Dixon Line." This is true. Our nearest neighbor, Jewel Ann Crenshaw, adopted Puffy from the pound after the death of her husband. Puffy was a six-pound Yorkie mix who had hated me ever since I turned the garden hose on her when I was sixteen. Doing the math, the mutt had to have found the Fountain of Doggie Youth.

The dog looks in the direction of Jewel Ann, then back to me, its top lip quivering in anticipation. I raise my hands a few inches from my sides like Gary Cooper before a gunfight. "Hello, Puffy, you ugly little motherfucker."

A firm hand on my shoulder startles me back to reality.

"It is a thing of woe." Fanny blows her nose into a handkerchief.

I'm not sure if she's crying or not. "Yeah, well, let's don't dive off a burning bridge just yet," I say, giving her a hug.

"I taught you that," she says without a lick of sentiment. The only wrinkle in her face is a near-straight line between her big dark eyes. A single strand of gray swoops across the top of her coal-black shoulder-length hair. She takes my hand.

I indicate the dog still standing guard like a sentinel at hell's gates. "Is this—I mean, this *can't* be—"

"Puffy." Fanny sniffs.

"But—"

"Number Three."

"Gotcha," I say, wondering how I missed Number Two.

Fanny points to the sunroom straight ahead. Through the spotless panes, I can see Tina perched on a stool on the brick patio.

I tiptoe across the wooden sundeck for a closer look at her before I announce myself. When Tina is really plugged into her painting, she squints at the canvas until her eyes appear closed, like what she's seeing is too vivid to take in with her naked eye.

"Hi," I finally say.

Tina squints over the canvas and smiles the way she always did, as if doubting the world would smile back. "Hi," she says. She puts down her brush and walks over. Although the two of us are facing each other, neither of us makes a move to embrace. I think we both feel it may be too much on the both of us. Her hair, colored a natural-looking brunette, is cut short and stylish with lighter highlights, a trick that makes her come off freshly scrubbed and youthful. I take her hands in mine. "Hey."

She sighs, another smile. "It all started with a cough," she says, as if she still can't believe she has inoperable lung cancer and is standing here in the middle of this seemingly perfect day. "I was having trouble on my walks, you know, climbing the hills? They checked my heart, took an X-ray, everything was fine. Few weeks later, they took another X-ray and found it. Doctor even called me at home to tell me I had lung cancer. Didn't even ask whether or not I was by myself, which I was." Tina looks to the sky and points. "Did you see these clouds?" she says, squinting. "Look, there's a giraffe! Or is it a bird?"

I take Tina in my arms and hug her tight. She seems smaller, thinner, like some kind of bird herself. She pulls back and studies my face.

"There's the big city boy."

My father's voice blasts from the patio steps behind me. Unlike my mother, my father had not once visited me in the sixteen years since I had left. Tina turns me to face him like it's my first day of school. Garrett slaps my belly with the back of his hand. "Getting a little soft there, huh?"

I know I'm supposed to find humor in the remark, but I don't. "I guess. You look…" I say, trying to sort out a compliment for this man I always thought so much more handsome than me.

"Still one ninety-five, stripped," he says, puffing his chest and slapping his belly.

I'm trying to remember whether or not we shook hands or hugged the last time we greeted each other when I notice Sis standing directly behind him, dressed in her Sunday best like Garrett. "We were at a funeral," she says, giving me a quick hug. "Ginny Ezell's sister. You remember her?"

"Nuh-uh."

"So," Sis says, going to retrieve my luggage, "are you here to take over?"

"No."

"Yes, he is," Tina says with a wink, her eyes never leaving mine.

11

I brought books. Lots and lots of books." I speak carefully and purposefully in what my father calls my brogue, the clipped Standard American English one learns in speech class the first semester of college to keep prospective employers north of the Mason-Dixon Line from branding you a halfwit. The blades of the overhead fans keep a lazy downbeat for the cicadas outside the sunroom. I recorded the sound on my first trip home from L.A., something to drown out the din of my apartment complex neighbors fucking and fighting in languages I'd never heard.

"Tina," I say from the white birch love seat in the corner. Tina snaps to attention, her tiptoes halting the basket swing, a decorating fiasco from the seventies. I grab *You Can Heal Yourself* from the carry-on by my side and hold it next to my face.

"The theory is we cause our disease through our thinking," I tell her, feeling my heartbeat in my ears. "Lung cancer can actually be caused by holding in our true feelings."

Garrett and Sis, perched on identical rockers, are looking anywhere but at me. Tina stares blankly at the book. "Good God, has it always been this hot down here?" I say, mopping the flop sweat from the back of my neck with a tissue. Tina takes the book. Sis rolls her eyes. Garrett pushes an unruly lock of silvery mane from his face, the result of too many three-dollar haircuts from Frank Whitman, an elderly barber who should have been forcefully retired from service years ago.

"You know what, punkin?" Garrett says to Tina. "I've had a cancer policy on you since we were married. If a medicine or a procedure costs whatever, the policy'll pay that amount, plus they'll pay us again the same amount for our trouble." He shoves another fistful of white hair over his ear with a prideful glance at Tina, who smiles and lightly touches Garrett's knee in silent thanks.

"Well," I say, grabbing another book from the carry-on, trying to retain control of the situation, "that's good to know. But it would be really great if we could rely on Western medicine as little as possible. I mean, I know you've decided on having the chemo, Tina, but still..." I stall for a moment before finally stepping into the wobbly abyss. "Sis, read this—*Recovery*—about a woman with lung cancer who heals herself with macrobiotics."

Sis, now the size of a twig and looking so much like her mother, takes the book and fans herself with it. "This isn't one of those California things, is it?"

"No," I say, like she'd asked if it was a treatise on devil worshipping. "It is not."

"Good. 'Cause if it *is*—"

"It is not one of those California things. Now." I wave another book through the thick, sultry air, this one a tome of almost eight hundred pages, perhaps not the best choice. "Macrobiotic philosophy teaches cancer is caused by an imbalance in the body brought on by unbalanced eating."

Swatting an invisible mosquito, I check their reactions. Sis picks a broken nail, Garrett yawns, and Tina chews her bottom lip in concentration. "This diet requires a great deal of study and preparation. It yields best results under a completely controlled organic environment." I turn to a glass-eyed Garrett and proceed with caution. "Garrett. I'm g-g-going to *have* to teach you how to cook." I pray my father doesn't notice I actually stuttered like I did for a short time when I was five.

Garrett rolls his eyes at Sis, then sets his sights back on me. "Are you sure this isn't one of those California things, Skeeter?"

"It is NOT one of those California things!" I say, standing, unconsciously caving in to my need to feel bigger than them at this moment. "It is Japanese. Way, waaaaay across the Pacific far, far away from anything California. Okay?" The mosquito truck backfires, heading up the hill in front of the house. Everyone jumps like a bomb went off. For a split second, I think how much easier it would be if I were instead attempting to soothe a roomful of egomaniacal Hollywood hotheads.

I check my list on a nearby end table and sit back down. "Now. In the next couple of days, I'm going to completely rid the whole place of all household chemicals. No pesticides, polishes, or cleaners. We can make our own soaps and shampoos."

Garrett says "Ha." Sis snorts. Tina masks a smile of mortified intrigue, stealthily watching Garrett and Sis's reactions.

"Tina," I say, "there's a couple who teach at a place in Tennessee. It's a community of people, not really a commune."

"Commune?" Tina says. "In Tennessee?"

"Well, it's a ten-hour drive. It's a weekend thing. If you're up for it."

"Commune," Garrett says. "Isn't that—"

"It is *not*—" I snap, slapping the same mosquito hard on the back of my neck. "*Shit!*"

Tina winces.

"Watch your mouth," Garrett says.

"Sorry."

"Commune," Garrett says to Sis, and they both snort. Tina has pulled her blouse up around her throat, attempting to disappear.

"Some sort of sex camp," Sis says, trying to catch her breath from a deadly case of the giggles.

Snatching a moment to clear the air, I glance around the room at nothing in particular. But all eyes are still on me, everyone waiting for another punch line. Garrett and Sis exchange another look before breaking into hysterical laughter.

"Well," I say, my voice cracking. "I think it could be a good thing," I say, trying to keep Tina's focus.

"Commune," Sis says.

Rattled, my face flushed with heat, I scooch down on the Mexican tiled floor and quietly ask for a cold, damp cloth for my face.

Later that night, as I'm finally drifting off in my room at the end of the hall, I feel my father's hand tousle my hair. It isn't the only time I've felt it since my childhood, as it has become a practice reserved solely for the first night of my visits.

I know the day will come when I'll miss it.

THE DIXIE

May 16, 1999
<u>Crime</u> <u>Scene</u>

In the past few weeks, Clarke County residents have been entertained by reports of a nude man living it up next to the county's busiest road. In one case, a caller said he was wearing a cap and sneakers. The next one said he was only wearing a fishing shirt. Local pundits have dubbed him the Naked Man, and he seems to be working his way into local legend. Many are doubting his existence, even after Deputy Larry Jay Motts claimed to have discovered the man pulling on his pants across the street from the old drive-in movie theatre on Highway 43 just before he disappeared behind the snack bar. "It doesn't make sense," Kristy Kelp, owner of the Walker Springs Grab & Go says. "Streaking went out thirty years ago. What could he be thinking?" Fruitlessly trailing the Naked Man down a logging road and through PeeWee Rivers's gravel pit, Motts and his fellow deputies said they could tell from his footprints he was moving pretty fast.

12

S o, here's this," I say, handing Tina the brochure. The two of us are perched on the creek's bank, soothing our feet in the icy water at the bottom of the hollow behind the house. Thankfully, I am considerably more calm and collected this time around, with nary a heckler in sight. "There are macrobiotic counselors all over the world. They're like natural foods physicians. The closest one is the Village in Knoxville, Tennessee. Run by a husband and wife team, Justin and Marsala Rosen, it's a base camp bed-and-breakfast nestled in the foothills of the Smoky Mountains National Park. There are six other houses on the property. We can take the scenic route," I say, trying to gauge her final reaction to my hard sell. "So. Are you up for it?"

Tina smiles and takes my hand.

❖

I am standing with my mother on the sundeck of the expansive mountain home, nervous and energized by the alien surroundings. On the hill beyond the house, a handful of people are harvesting something green from neatly tended rows in a garden. A life-sized granite statue of a woman with a gigantic vulva stands on the far end of the sundeck. I feel as though I've stepped into the cover of a gorgeously illustrated box of raisins.

An older man, stooped and cheery with dyed auburn hair, answers the door, smiles, and greets us in a big, booming voice. "Weeelcome to the Village. My name is Justin. I'm the only Jew in a tri-county area. There will be time for pictures later. Ha!"

Tina looks at me with a big fake smile.

Justin eyes the harvesters and rings a dinner bell mounted on the wall next to the door before stepping aside. "Please. Come in. Kindly remove your shoes. It deposits all the outside *chi* on the doorstep."

We enter and take off our flip-flops, leaving them next to a fat yellow cat snoozing in the sun. Justin smiles, nods, farts, and turns. Tina and I follow him to a cluttered desk in the corner of the rustic glass room overlooking the mountains. "One thousand for the weekend includes your own rooms on the property here and all meals prepared by us," he says. A plain, barefooted woman enters, whisks away our flip-flops, and disappears. "It also includes a counseling session to get you started." Justin trails off into another part of the house. Tina and I hustle to keep up.

❖

Ten or so students of all ages, sizes, and ethnicities are standing at the long wooden dining table set with chopsticks and Japanese soup bowls. Everyone smiles at the two of us. We nod back nervously as the remnants of an early evening thunderstorm fire one last flash of electricity over a mountain that looks like a pyramid in the encroaching darkness. A gray-haired woman of seventy motions for us all to sit.

Justin stands at the head of the table, acknowledging the gray-haired woman on the other end. "This is my wife, Marsala." Marsala nods as Tina and I take our seats on the benches. Justin introduces the assorted dishes on the table like Ed Sullivan announcing his enviable guest lineup: "This is brown rice with millet, adzuki beans with chestnuts, steamed kale, and," he says, more playfully here, "hijiki sea vegetable. First, the grace." Justin sits, farts, and bows his head.

Clearly, beans was Justin's macrobiotic protein of choice.

Tina stifles a laugh and tries not to look at me as Justin begins. "O universe, we thank you for this well-balanced meal. For the farmers who grew it and the distributors who brought it to our table." He nods at Tina and me through one squinted eye. "For friends in our home, and most importantly, for our teachers—Michio and Aveline Kushi at the Kushi Institute in Beckett, Massachusetts—for bringing this wonderful lifestyle into our midst. Amen." Everyone smiles in agreement as they pass bowls from left to right.

Tina clears her throat to address our two hosts. "Well, I agree with the Bible that the Jews are God's chosen people."

Looking for something to do besides screaming "WHAAAT??" to my mother like a bug-eyed cartoon character, I attempt to change the subject. Glancing dramatically into a nearby pot with a tiny gasp, I raise both eyebrows in gleeful anticipation at the sight of something stewed and orange.

"Thank you, Tina," Justin says pleasantly. "My wife isn't Jewish, though. Marsala was raised Catholic."

"But I consider myself Presbyterian," Marsala says, offering Tina a bowl of brown, squishy discs. "Lotus ball?" Tina takes the bowl and looks inside as Marsala prattles on. "I've seen macrobiotics change so many people's lives. Why, it's brought Justin and me glory and riches beyond anything we'd ever…" Marsala is suddenly lost.

Everyone looks respectfully into their laps as Marsala attempts to remember the rest of her train of thought. She shivers and whimpers twice like a tired Chihuahua.

Justin interjects. "My wife had a mini-stroke some years ago. She gets lost, but never you fear, she'll find her way back."

And she does. "It's really quite impressive, the things you see," Marsala says. "People healing themselves of advanced stage cancers, like Gina, here."

Gina, sixty-something, stops slurping her soup long enough to smile through questionable dental work.

Marsala plows ahead. "Careers turning around for the first time, relationships blossoming. You see, when you're eating according to the natural laws, you experience a spiritual, mental, and physical clarity so that all the bullshit you've allowed in your lives is finally recognized and..." With another whimper, she's lost again.

Justin takes over with gusto. "Seaweed fajita, anybody?"

❖

"You okay?" I ask, entering Tina's tiny brown paneled room. Japanese art with fat naked Japanese people wrestling and screwing adorns the walls; overstuffed pillows and warm-colored throws are tossed haphazardly in every available corner. Vaguely remembering some ridiculous Don Knotts movie I'd seen as a kid where he was a reluctant guru to a band of hippies, I'm suddenly wondering if it's too late to get us both out.

Tina brushes her hair contentedly in front of a small vanity. "Well, I suppose they're both very nice," she whispers, "if a little excitable." Holding back her hair from her face, she checks the effect in the mirror. "The view is breathtaking." I'm taken aback by her apparent newfound narcissism until I realize she's talking about the mountains. "I think I could live up here if it weren't so far out in the wilderness," she says, taking my hand, sitting me on the bunk bed next to her. "Hey, whoever thought I'd be eating with chopsticks, huh? But I suppose Justin is right, they are a more peaceful utensil." Tina takes in a quick breath of astonishment. "And what about getting rid of all the electrical appliances, even the stove? I mean, I haven't cooked on gas since...Oh, and giving up the television? What will your father do without Fox News?" She gets up and rummages through her overnight bag on the chest of drawers. "So. The consultation is tomorrow. Marsala said she would examine me. Do you know they can tell where your cancer is just by looking at you?" She glances out the window once more, this time like a kid pondering Christmas. "Yes, there's definitely healing in the air here."

❖

While I am seated with the rest of the students on the sundeck atop the mountain, Marsala stands directly behind Tina on a sort of outcropping, a round, stage-like area over the steepest part of the canyon. I'm thinking if we were in L.A., this back porch in the clouds would be the last place I'd wanna be during a killer quake.

Marsala positions Tina so that she's in full view of the group, her hands on either side of Tina's face. "See this redness on the upper cheeks? That's Tina's lung cancer. As she continues on the diet, this will begin to vanish. Do you tend to hold things inside?" Marsala asks Tina.

"Well…" Tina clears her throat.

Marsala walks Tina around the sundeck, parading her in front of the rest of the eager students like a first-class specimen. "Most lung cancer patients do. I'm going to recommend you scrub your entire body from head to toe every morning with fresh ginger. This will rid your system of the chemotherapy when you begin your treatments. I also want to teach you how to breathe." Marsala points to Tina's diaphragm. "From *here*," she says, "not from your chest. Now. Would you like your son to leave the area before we discuss your sex life?"

Tina glances sheepishly in my direction. Unlike all my friends' parents, my parents' sex life was still terrific. The bedroom was probably the one place where they still communicated and communicated well. I know this because my father has always insisted on giving me unsolicited booty call reports. "Well, I'm still liking that stuff a coupla times a week. And I usually get it, too. And half the time, it's your mama's idea!" Many were the nights when, home for the holidays, I would come home from a night of carousing to spy their bathroom light aglow as I drove into the carport, a sure sign since my youth not to come a knockin'.

I wave goodbye to Tina in haste, tripping over the fat yellow cat as I make my way awkwardly down the sundeck stairs.

❖

With a new lease on life, we return to the Gulf Coast from this hallowed place where happy, skinny people in hemp wear and Birkenstocks spoke of spontaneous healings and miraculous conversions.

Two mornings later, Garrett and Sis watch frozen from the kitchen window as I direct an old pickup loaded with shiny appliances down the driveway and out onto Blue Cove Road. Jewel Ann Crenshaw, now eighty-five and looking every minute of it, studies me from across the road with two other blue-haired biddies, waving cheerily, their faces a trio of question marks. I wave good-naturedly and go back inside, barely catching the word "California" in a disparaging tone from their vicinity.

I recall a story I'd heard on the radio about an old dying man whose son comes home with a miracle cure he'd completely fabricated. But because of his faith in the boy, the old man actually got better and lived well for ten more years. Little did we know one of the biggest challenges lying in wait would be something as basic as sustenance, and where the devil to find it.

❖

Tina and I peer skeptically through a dingy window on the backside of Fairlane Plaza, a near-deserted shopping center in Mobile long past its prime. Healthy Way Foods, one of the only natural foods stores in a sixty-mile radius, hunkers down between

Oasis Bible Book Store and an abandoned establishment quietly heralding Adult Videos across a blacked-out door. We brace ourselves for the worst and step inside.

Tina follows me down a row of sad-looking bulk items: dried lima beans, a paltry mound of wheat flour, a few sad grains of brown rice. As I pull a package of mystery noodle from the shelf and blow off a cloud of dust, Tina wrinkles her nose.

A wormy manager changes a fluorescent bulb from a wobbly stepladder at the end of the row.

"Excuse me," I say, "do you have any quinoa?"

"Quin-*what*?"

"Quin-*oa*. It's a grain."

"Not that I know of," he says, uninterested.

Tina looks at me and shrugs. "Let's just go."

"You're not sure," I say, spellbound by the dense dusting manager who's already forgotten us.

The manager mumbles over his shoulder. "You can look around. Some of this stuff has been here for years."

"Well, that much is clear," I snort.

Tina tugs on my shirt sleeve. "It's okay, Bo Skeet, let's go."

I watch the manager for a moment longer, dusting his little cans in a miasma of ignorance.

Tina motions once more for me to come along, but something deep inside me breaks. I feel like I can scrape all the indifference in the world off this pinhead with my fingernails. Tina looks worried.

"Let's try this again, shall we? Hello. Phillip Stalworth." I say my name like it's a hallowed celebrity handle, holding out my hand for him to reach down and shake, which he finally does. "What's *your* name?"

"Glen," he says, like he's not quite sure.

"You know, Glen, there's not a lot here for a health food store. I mean, where's the seaweed, huh?" I ask, hauling something off the shelf I'm not certain how to pronounce. "I mean, sure, here's some out-of-date kombu, " I say, tossing the package back on the shelf, "but where's the nori? That's standard for *any* macrobiotic diet."

Making my way back to the manager, who has made no move to continue his bulb-changing, I come in for the close. "Now. We're not gonna be your run-of-the-mill customers who come in once a month for a jug of vitamins and a carton of soy milk," I say, looking over at Tina, who has planted herself invisibly next to a rusty display rack of lo-fat carrot chips. "We're gonna be in here on a daily basis, understand?" I say with a nod to Tina before looking back to the manager. "We're gonna be needing everything, okay? We will be spending thousands upon thousands of dollars, okay?"

The manager finally offers up a firm "Okay."

"So," I say, crossing my arms across my chest, "how long you think it'll take you to get some of that seaweed in here?"

❖

My family gathers around the rambling cherrywood table in the anodyne dining room, a place still reserved solely for birthdays and Christian holidays. The most Tina and I have gotten from my father on the TV front is for him to agree to turn off the set at mealtimes. The table is laden with an impressive array of fresh grains and vegetables, the colorful spread bathed in the glow of nontoxic dinner candles. Garrett and Sis look on impatiently as I enter with another dish. Wiping my hands on my apron, I skirt past their backsides and take a seat next to Tina, who grins at me in approval. Sis crosses her arms across her chest as Tina passes a bowl to a suspicious Garrett.

"I still don't know *why* we have to eat seaweed," Sis says.

"Does smell kinda like cat pee," Garrett says, sampling a taste with his fingers. "But it's really not so bad."

Tina takes a whiff of the sea veggie. "I told you all if you wanted to go by Kentucky Fried, then—"

"So the seaweed thing is just *what*?" Sis says.

"It's supposed to be full of nutrients and vitamins," Tina says.

"Well," Sis grins, "so is field dirt but you won't see me making cornbread out of it."

Sis tries to get a fellow rise out of Garrett, but he's already on his second helping of dulse. Sis raises a finger. "And another question—"

I drop the dish I'm currently passing with a thud. "For God's sake, you don't have to eat the seaweed!" I say, my voice getting too high for comfort. "Just—God. You know, I'm not your little brother anymore. That was a long time ago and now I'm just—"

"Calm down," Sis says, like I'm the one who started it.

Tina grabs my hand and bows her head. "Oh, God," I begin like there's a gun to my head. I remember to loosen my shoulders and breathe. "We thank you for this well-balanced meal, for the farmers who grew it, for the distributors who brought it to the table, and most importantly, for our teachers—Justin and Marsala Rosen, at the Village in Townsend, Tennessee—for bringing this wonderful lifestyle into our midst. Amen."

Sis leans in my direction and whispers. "And you will *always* be my little brother. Pass the seaweed, please, Garrett."

13

VAN HALEN FOR PRESIDENT. I study the white decal still plastered to the inner reaches of the rolltop desk Garrett bought for me as a study incentive when I was twelve. The decals, obtained from the rock group's fan club, were handed out by a few of us to the student body of my alma mater, the University of Montevallo, in protest of Ronald Reagan's imminent sweep of the White House in '81. The remaining contents of the desk, a crystalline arrowhead I found on a Boy Scout camping trip, a tiny photo of Billy Wade, Patience and me at a high school toga party, and a set of rattles from a snake my father killed with a stick on my sixteenth birthday, have been pushed to the back to make way for the things Garrett accumulated during his tenure in the business world: a picture of him shaking hands with pharmaceutical bigwigs on a ship somewhere, the name plate from his desk—GARRETT BOYD STALWORTH—and the gold Rolex he received at thirty years of service.

You've got mail.

I glance at my laptop, a token from Frances on my first day of service, and find two other messages from Her Highness. Frances's idea of being respectful of my time here entails calling me no more than three times a day and emailing me no less than fifty. Ignoring the emails, I open my writing program and stare at the blank page.

I'd told friends on more than one occasion I'd never felt anything of consequence had ever happened to me. Despite half a life lived in Tinseltown, I'd never reaped the benefits of any substantial achievement. No long-term relationship, no job satisfaction, no real home to hang my hat. After reaching into the top desk drawer for my secret stash of SweeTarts, I place the roll of candy next to my laptop and type this sentence:

Yesterday morning I awoke in a self-sustained cooperative in the foothills of the Great Smoky Mountains.

Several minutes pass before I type the next sentence and, in some sort of involuntary act of rebellion, toss the SweeTarts into the trash.

❖

With my encouragement, Tina became obsessed with the lifestyle. Justin and Marsala cut out all bread, meat, sugar, and dairy, and Tina investigated anything she could dig up on macrobiotics. Driving away one Sunday, Justin and Marsala waved from the Village. "Drive carefully! You're in the fold now. Wild and wonderful things will begin to happen!"

And they did.

I have been a runner since reading Jim Fixx's book as a senior in high school, just before he died of a heart attack during an afternoon jog. Although the incident placed the fear of God in me for months, the fact that running had allowed me to unload the thirty pounds of baby fat I had still been carrying keeps me running to this day.

When one jogs in the heat and humidity that is the Deep South, the goal is to always be done before the rising sun changes the surface of the Tombigbee from ochre to silver. To finish any later would be dancing with the same devil that took Jim out of this world. Like a day had never passed, I grab my shoes by the sunroom entrance and dash through the carport, trying my damndest to make it past Jewel Ann's front porch before Puffy rouses herself from old dog slumber.

Pushing as hard as I can up the biggest hill on Blue Cove Road, I spy her from the corner of my eye, sleeping on the mat at the top of the old wooden steps. I entertain the possibility that she may not even be lucid before noon. "Hello, Puffy," I say, under my breath like a warning, "you ugly little motherfucker."

She bolts, nipping my heels in no time with a series of threatening wheezy yips.

"Pig-eyed piece of shit," I say, remembering how, even though the varmint's attacks rarely drew blood, they hurt like hell and threatened to sabotage one of the few joys in my life. Attempting to block out the ruckus, I remember poor dead Jim's advice to move effortlessly, hands at your side, as if pulling your way on a fixed rope. I feel a slight pain in my chest and wonder if Jim's final run around the track started like this, until I hear Jewel Ann's voice cracking under the hill, "HEEEEERE, PUFFYPUFFYPUFFY!"

And that, at least for the present, takes care of that.

❖

"HEY, *HOLLYWOOD!*" A baritone voice startles me out of my endorphin-induced contemplation as I run back through my parents' neck of the woods. "OVER HERE!"

Running in place, I track movement atop the bare-bones frame of a house camouflaged by a row of cedars straight ahead. A lone figure in jeans and a T-shirt waves his hammer in my direction from atop a second story of construction scaffolding. Shielding my eyes from the rising sun, I jog tentatively down the oyster shell driveway.

"Hey, how far do you run, anyway?" The lanky carpenter flashes an amiable smile from underneath a Braves baseball cap, a sign he must have connections at New Era, a local factory making hats for major league baseball teams. Although the public was occasionally allowed to purchase a few of the caps, the Braves had always been a hard commodity to come by.

"Did you hear me?" he says, "I asked you how far—"

"I heard you," I shout. One of the most maddening things about going home again is dealing with those who, since they never left, remember high school like it was yesterday. Everyone recognizes you, but you remember no one. "I'm not sure," I say, hoping that much will suffice so I can get on with my constitutional.

Braves Cap waves his hammer in my direction and leans across the top of the door frame below him. "I heard you were back in these parts. You got killed in some soap opera, right?"

"Yup," I say, pushing down the familiar shame of failure.

"What's that?"

I clear my throat and say it a bit louder. "I did, yes, that was me."

"Well," he says, painfully earnest. "I suppose one could coast on something like that for quite some time."

"I'm sorry. Do I know you?"

"Hey, you're making me dizzy," he says, pitching a nail into the side of his mouth for safekeeping.

"Huh?"

Braves points his hammer at my still-jogging feet.

"Oh, sorry," I say, making a feeble attempt to stand still.

"So. You don't remember me," he says, holding up a level to a two-by-four. "At all."

Since my only available sightline consists of a straight shot up the legs of his shorts, I study the row of red-berried nandinas to my left, nudging my memory one last time. "I'm—nu-uh," I mumble.

"I was a couple years ahead of you," he says, removing his cap for a moment, "but I was in public school, and I had more hair back then. We lived on Main Street."

I study the carpenter again. He's more than a bit handsome,

still a pretty impressive head of black hair from where I stand, only a few grays in sight. Still drawing a blank on the face slightly craggy from too many days in the sun, I shrug, shaking my head with a half-smile.

"*Still* no?" he says, like a disappointed child.

I shrug again, and he drops the hammer, leaps down from the frame and circles me, dribbling an invisible ball. Heading to the phantom net on the nearby poplar, he jumps, torso twisted behind him. "He shoots, *scores*! Two points for the Jackson Bobcats!" he hollers, with just a hint of desperation.

I say it fast like a forgotten mantra: "Irondick Tischman?"

He laughs, pulling the cap down over his eyes. "Well, there's a name I don't hear anymore." He sticks out his hand. "The name's Joe."

I shake, embarrassed, temporarily lost in the recollection his visual had conjured up of countless Friday nights sitting in the stands, the legion of Bobcats fans chanting the salacious moniker for one of Coach Benton's golden boys. The origin of said nickname was unknown except to a few seniors who weren't talking, at least to us pathetic underlings. More than once, Gleason Hadley, the principal, threatened to stop the proceedings mid-game if the licentious chanting wasn't curtailed.

"Yeah, sure," I say, still pumping his hand, "Joe. Right."

"It's okay. Old habits die hard." He sits on the ground beside me, one of the few folks I've seen get more good-looking with the passage of time. "I was sorry to hear, you know, about your mom."

"Right. Thanks," I say, looking up into the branches of the poplar, the underbelly of the emerald leaves silver dollars in the breeze.

Joe etches nothing in the dirt with a crooked pine stick.

"So," I say, pointing to the skeleton of the home in front of me.

"Oh, this," he says, turning around. "My folks' place. They bought it a couple of years ago. Now it's pretty much a casualty of the last big storm. They're in Gulf Shores while I do what I do."

The endless barrage of hurricanes through the Gulf Coast breeds tornados like rabbits. After the most recent, Garrett had called me in California to brag about standing just outside the cellar door, hanging on for dear life while watching as a series of twisters curled down Blue Cove Road like giant Slinkys.

"Is that yours?" I say, pointing to a family-sized camp tent pitched under an old chinaberry behind the house.

"Yeah. Just till I get the walls up. Come on, I'll give you a tour of the first floor, since that's all we've got yet." He waves over my shoulder in the direction of the road behind me. "Hey, isn't that your dad?"

I turn around to see Garrett staring curiously through the windshield of his pickup at the two of us. No doubt he's headed to the "coffee-drankin'," an appointment he's kept for decades at Joe Brown's Pharmacy, the insides of which don't appear to have changed since the war, probably the first one. "That's him," I say, remembering I've forgotten to grill the tempeh for today's lunch.

"So what about that tour?"

"No thanks," I say, finding my idling pace again. "You take care." I round the poplar before making my way back down the driveway to the road below. "Good seeing you." I wave once over my shoulder, glancing back at the small-time basketball hero before he disappears behind the wall of cedars.

THE DIXIE

June 7, 1999
Out & About

Alisia Jenks Nabs First Deer of Season

Alisia Jenks, 6, daughter of Ken and Heather Jenks, killed the first deer of the hunting season. Alisia took down the twelve-point buck with a twelve-gauge, a gift from her grandparents for her fifth birthday. As per custom, the little tyke was paraded through town early Saturday morning, her face painted with the blood of the beast. This marks the second year in a row the first deer was bagged by one of our younger hunters. Last year, Jimmy Connell, 8, took the honors. Come on, old folks, let's not let the young'uns show us up too bad! Congrats, Alisia!

14

A re you in?" I say as Tina situates herself in the front seat of the Lincoln with a nod. Slamming the door behind her, I go around to the other side and hop in behind the wheel. Already in the back seat, Sis is checking herself in the window's reflection. Garrett watches condescendingly from the carport. Tina tries her best to ignore him. "Have you ever seen a look like that? Like we're disappearing into the pages of a Stephen King novel with the witches and the goblins and the headless everybodies."

"I'm not so sure we're not," Sis says, popping her Juicy Fruit, a newfound habit to replace the smokes.

I start the engine and turn the air conditioner on full blast. "Just try not to look at him."

Tina examines herself in the sun visor mirror and purses her lips. "Well, Fanny says this fellow comes highly recommended."

Sis hoots from the back seat. "A ringing endorsement."

❖

A woman who looks like a "Touch Me in the Morning"–era Diana Ross waves sleepily from the entrance of a narrow dirt road.

"You can walk in from here," she says, leaning into Tina's open window.

Honest to God, I can see three bats dip just behind her in the summer heat.

"Are we doing this?" Sis asks sheepishly, the only time to my mind she's ever asked *anything* sheepishly.

"Hellpecker *yes*," I say opening the car door, feeling a bit sheepish myself.

❖

The bonfire in back of the ramshackle shotgun house casts a supernatural glow across Tina, prostrate on a long, wooden table next to a grinning human skull and a copy of the New Testament. Scattered items of junk have been fashioned into art around the riverside abode: a mile-high stack of wrought iron patio chairs, clearly inspired by the Watts Towers, peers over the proceedings, while a life-sized aluminum Christmas angel hangs like a lynching victim from a tattered rope in a nearby pine. A pair of African American children playing in a burned-out Chevy make me think of survivors in a TV miniseries I'd seen about the apocalypse.

Brother Peter, a tall West Indian standing across the table from me, holds his thick, ancient hands out over Tina's body and motions for me to do the same. He locks his eyes into mine like he's trying to read my thoughts.

"Okay, you feel de heat?"

"Yeah," I say, definitely feeling something. "I feel it."

His gaze suggests I'm in over my head. "Heezzzzzbokmon," he hisses.

A cockeyed parrot squawks from its perch just behind my head. Flinching like a whipped hound, I make a gallant attempt to recover.

"Nooooow," he says, "to make your hands into de wings of a dove."

Taking his lead, I fan out my hands in front of me like the feathers of something he'll find acceptable.

"HEEZBOKMON!" No hiss this time, more like an outright holler.

"Bo Skeet—" Sis says from her lawn chair underneath the Christmas angel.

"*Silence*, sister!" Brother Peter shuts her down hard without a glance in her direction.

The parrot squawks, and I hurriedly change the shape of my hands into something less incendiary.

"Okay now, mooove it to de left."

I follow Brother Peter's giant shadow as we move our hands to the left, his forceful eyes following me from across the table. "HEEZBOKMON! *HEEZBOKKK!*"

The parrot dances on its perch, flapping its wings like someone's trying to kill it.

"HEEZBOKMON!"

My tipping point.

"What are you saying?" I say, downright panicked. "I don't know what that means, and you keep yelling it at me!"

Sis whispers behind my ear. "*Ease back, man.*"

"What?" I say, wary as hell of speaking to anyone but Brother Peter.

With her hands on my shoulders, Sis moves me back an inch. "You need to ease back."

"Ease back," Tina whispers, like we're all on our way to the principal's office.

"Oh," I say, relieved someone finally broke the foreign dialect code. "Ease back. Right." Still too petrified to look our fearless leader in the eye, I carefully take two steps back, my hands still over Tina's chest. From my peripheral vision, I can see Brother Peter offering a tiny nod of affirmation.

"Heezebok," I say, and this time I mean it.

❖

Brother Peter walks us to the car, no flunky in sight, his hand on Tina's back. Although he is addressing my mother in soft tones, Sis and I are able to hear every word. "Pray, meditate, whatever it is you do. But do it twice a day. Concentrate on one thing that gives you power. Do this religiously. If you do this thing I'm telling you, the powers of darkness won't have room to get in. Do you understand?"

"Yes," my mother says.

We are now at the car. Brother Peter and Tina are facing each other. He takes both her hands in his.

"Say that you understand, but use your voice where I can hear it," he says.

"Yes," Tina says, louder. "I understand you."

"Say your name. Your first name."

"Tina."

"Again."

"*Tina*," she says a bit louder.

"Again."

"TINA!" she says, like a town crier.

Brother Peter smiles and opens the passenger door. "Every single day," he says.

Tina gets in the car. "Tina." She says it one more time and smiles as he closes the door.

When we are all finally tucked away in the car, I look over at my mother, who is blushing like a bride.

"Tina," she says, glancing out the window at the place where Brother Peter had just stood.

❖

The big blue lights of the Highway 43 Chevron Station signals our late-night return to civilization. Tina has tuned the radio to cool jazz. Sis lies across the back seat, asleep for all we know.

"Okay, Sis," Tina says. "It's time to come clean. Fanny told me."

"Told you what?"

Tina turns around. "You found Brother Peter, not Fanny."

I can hear Sis sit up. "Well, no."

"You didn't?"

"Melanie Pugh mentioned him," Sis says. "He led a prayer circle for her daddy. So, I mentioned him to Fanny and she said she'd met him a couple of times and thought he was the real deal. So—"

"You asked Fanny to take the fall in case it turned out to be a bust."

Sis looks out the window. "You could say that."

Tina holds her hand over the seat for Sis to take. "It wasn't a bust, Sis."

"Well, you just never know," Sis says, taking her mother's hand.

The sense of pride and anticipation in the car is palpable.

15

Sis follows me, still sweaty from my run, up the ladder of the remnants of the ancient tree house. Even as an older, albeit misfit teen, I'd often come in from school and climb the ladder, pretending I was Alan Ladd in *Shane* come to save the sodbusters and their helpless families from Jack Palance and the other evil cattlemen. I'd hold a hand over one eye, like John Wayne's patch in *True Grit*, so I could never see what was coming from the left side of my face.

Although the evergreen paint has since peeled from the ladder steps and most of the walls have fallen victim to Gulf Coast weather, Garrett had the good sense to build the floor out of treated lumber, which is the only reason we could still go into the big, creaking room without taking our life in our hands.

Sis groans as she climbs the last two rungs. "If I break my neck on some rotten—"

"You're not gonna break your neck on some rotten," I say, pulling her into the house. With a pair of binoculars I've taken from Garrett's gun cabinet, I take a gander across the creek where Joe hammers particle board in the kitchen area of the Tischman house. "Here," I say, offering Sis the binoculars.

"What?" Sis swats the air around her, cursing an imaginary fly. "Shit."

"Remember Joe Tischman?"

"Irondick?" Sis squints into the binoculars and gasps. "Is *that* him?"

Tina climbs into the house, taking in her surroundings like a kid. "Who are we spying on?"

Sis says his name like something good to eat. "Joe Tischman."

"Two points, Jackson Bobcats," Tina says under her breath, shrugging her shoulders at my look of surprise at her uncanny recall. She leans her chin on the decaying banister and points the binoculars at the house across the creek. "Now, where'd he go to college? Ole Miss, I think."

I take the binoculars from Tina, offering up information like a first-time drunk. "He never went to college. He went to *India*. And everywhere else you can think of. Hitchhiking, climbing mountains. But eventually he came back here to build houses. He's very much in demand. He was in a bunch of magazines."

Sis gnaws a pine straw. "You heard, though, right?"

"What?" I say, following Joe's movement as he measures another particle board for cutting.

Tina takes back the binoculars. "His parents are in Gulf Shores. That's all I know."

"Janie Wright told me he went crazy," Sis says. "He lost it over there, went bonkers, whatever. Had to spend some time in Bryce or Searcy. One of those places."

Janie Wright's daddy, the Academy's only crossing guard, used to shoo imaginary colonies of ants off his feet while he ushered us from one side of the street to the other. Anything Janie Wright says, I take with a grain of salt.

Tina sits on the floor, hands me the binoculars, and hoists herself over the hatch. "Well, I'm glad you'll have somebody your own age to play with while you're here," she says, climbing back down the ladder.

Tina disappears down the hole, and Sis barks in pain from a splinter she's picked up from the wall of the tree house. "Ow, fuckit," she says, glancing in my direction.

I take her hand and find the splinter in her palm. It's a big one, easy to see.

"She's so happy you're here," Sis says.

"Well, I'm happy to be here."

"You are, aren't you? I mean, you don't mind?"

"No," I say, lifting the splinter. "It sort of worked out. It was a very good time to leave L.A."

"How's Caroline?" She takes her hand back. "Isn't that her name?"

"That's her name. And we're pretty much done. Like you, I hear?"

"Justine decided she wasn't gay. I was like, after seven years you need a label?" Sis drops to the floor and begins making her way back down the ladder. "People are crazy, aren't they?"

"They sure are," I say, glancing once more in the direction of Joe's house.

❖

Tina and I are seated in two identical overstuffed easy chairs. I am attempting to smile reassuringly, something I'm getting really good at.

A fleshy, sour-faced woman in her mid-fifties shuffles into the chemotherapy ward. Stooped and brittle, she barely acknowledges our presence. "My name's Rose O'Sharon, and I'll be your chemo nurse." I remember the same expression on the face of a rain-soaked possum I'd surprised while taking the trash out late one night. Rose O'Sharon trundles past us to a drawer behind my chair. "Mizrez Stalworth, I'll tell you what I tell all my stage four cancer patients. Hope for the best and prepare for the worst."

I take Tina's hand as if the act of doing so erases the fog of cruelty descending over the room.

"How's that grandbaby doin', Wanda?" she hollers at some unseen presence down the hall.

"Growin' like a weed," invisible Wanda hollers back.

"I'll swanee," Rose O'Sharon says, putting an end to the exchange, shuffling behind Tina's chair and holding up the bag hanging from an IV stand. "Now, I'll bring pamphlets," she says, "to answer anything I don't." She plows through her somber speech at lightning speed like she does it a thousand times a day. "This is carboplatin. This drug is particularly tough on the veins. It will eventually begin to eat them away."

The tragic excuse for a nurse sits on a stool across from Tina and takes her arm, and the matter at hand is under way before we know it. "It's also hard on the kidneys, so drink plenty of water. It kills the good blood cells with the bad blood cells, so if you come down with a fever or infection, get to a hospital immediately. It could prove fatal. Germs are now the number one enemy in your camp, so you must do everything in your power to keep them as far away from you as possible. Umph," she says, rising with a grunt before heading off to Pamphletland.

The first slo-mo drip of liquid poison drops from the plastic bag, and I'm thinking how the physical reality of the chemo itself seems hardly the stuff of nightmares. Just clear liquid and a needle.

Tina glances behind her chair at the bag. Her cheeks are rosy, and I remember what Justin and Marsala said about this being a symptom of the lung cancer. But this time they look rosier than ever, which makes me think the cancer is even more pissed off because the chemo is already beginning to kick its ass.

"Are you okay?" I say, kneeling in front of her.

She nods.

"Does it hurt?"

Tina shakes her head no.

"Great." I take a moment to chase out all the loathing I'm presently feeling for the way this business of living, loving, and dying is set up. "Do you mind if I lead us in a proactive spiritual exercise?" I say, citing one of Justin and Marsala's New Ageisms.

I get a weak smile from Tina as I put my arm behind her, closing my eyes, unsure how to begin.

"God?" I say, opening my eyes, unsatisfied with my paltry beginning. Glancing back at the bag hanging over my mother's head, feeling the weight of all that lies before us, I shut my eyes tight. This time I feel some indescribable endowment from the control freak deities. "GOD! We thank you for this beautiful waterfall of healing, heavenly light which is now making its way through Tina's body like a blowtorch of living energy completely annihilating any signs of cancerous growth in its thunderous path."

I search Tina's face for some sign of approval. "Are you all right?"

She nods and smiles.

I move closer like a quarterback in huddle, this time carefully coaxing, using words from an affirmation collection I'd found on my bedside table at the Village. "We realize the sentence of death is within ourselves. Which is why, in this moment, we choose—" I catch myself. "No. We gratefully *accept* light and life. Amen."

Glancing silently about the room, I notice what can only be a large puddle of pee in front of the easy chair by the door. Probably the last patient's knee-jerk reaction to some life-altering news. I make a mental note to lead Rose O'Sharon right through it on our way out.

❖

Although I came away from that day with a great deal more than I started out with, I had something taken away from me at the same time: my cavalier attitude towards germs.

The signs are instantaneous. It starts with doorknobs.

Tina and I exit the Lincoln and make our way through the carport. Pointing to the door, I make sure she understands the critical importance of Rose O'Sharon's warning. "Now. The door

to the Little House will *always* be opened with one's shirttail."
I demonstrate before we head to the entrance. "The gate to the
breezeway," I say, "with the underside of the forearm."

Proceeding to the sunroom, I sense a bit of playfulness
is called for at the French doors since Tina is becoming more
befuddled with every instruction. "French doorknob?" I say in
my worst Parisian accent, "back of ze hand." Turning around, I
open the door backward. Tina laughs as we proceed up the three
steps. "The last door to the mudroom?" I say in a high-pitched,
crazy voice. "SHIRTTAIL AGAIN!"

Garrett pokes his head around the corner and makes a face
full of vinegar.

"You think I'm kidding?" I say, spinning around.

Garrett narrows his eyes, and I grab Tina's hand, pulling her
quickly into the house.

❖

Tina knocks and enters at the same time. "Anybody home?"
I close my laptop and motion her into my bedroom.

"What are you working on? Tap, tap, tap. Like a woodpecker."

"Just emails and stuff."

"You know, I feel frightfully good," she says, sitting on
the edge of the bed. "Isn't that crazy? I think that extra dose of
seaweed and miso Justin and Marsala prescribed did the trick. I
mean, I think I'll still take the nausea pills, but—" She looks at
me with wide-eyed disbelief. "Boy, you sure came a long way
just for me. Thank you for reading all those books. And for all
those prayers today. If I'd been a cancer cell anywhere *near*
you I would have tucked my tail and run." She sits quietly for a
moment, biting a nail.

"Hey, punkin. You know what?" Garrett stops just outside
my bedroom door. He pushes the door open and leans into the
jamb, holding up a powder blue invoice of some sort, squinting
through his bifocals. "That chemo you're gonna be taking will

be costing upwards of three thousand dollars a month. 'Course it's not gonna cost us a dime with that old insurance policy I still carry on you. In fact, like I said, they'll be paying us a pretty penny on top of everything they reimburse, but still...crazy, right?" Garrett winks and goes back down the hall.

Tina glances up at the ceiling. "Well, I always wanted to be a financial contributor to this household. I just thought there were easier ways to go about it," she says. "But look at me," she says ironically, running a finger over the bandage from her chemo injection. "I'm a cash cow!" She giggles and shakes her head.

"Well, thank God somebody is," I say, taking her hand.

"Oh, which reminds me, your father left a book of checks in your top desk drawer over there, so at the beginning of every month, you can just send whatever you need out to your bank in California."

For a moment I'm sure I've heard her wrong. "I'm sorry, what did you say?"

"Your father said since you're not working, and you're helping *us* out, he thought he'd help *you* out. So." Tina looks at me like I have no reason to be surprised. And in truth, I don't. My parents have helped me out financially many times before. But the last time I was home, they finally said it was time I go down a different path. In fact, Tina had said tearfully, "I've seen you go through so much rejection, I wonder how much more my body and soul can take." It was one of the worst moments of my life, that time when those closest to you finally throw in the towel. Tina's words came back to haunt me after her diagnosis. *Did my life as a loser give my mother cancer?*

The cell phone vibrates on my bedside table, and Tina pats me on the knee. "You go on and get your phone call. It may be Frances." She walks over to the door. "See you in the funny papers." I still laugh every time she says it, just like when I was four.

16

The pool water feels like warm, wet cotton around my feet. My legs swing back and forth at the edge, where I've sprawled in the boxers and T-shirt I planned to crash in before I decided I was too wired to sleep. I can just make out the Seven Sisters over the Tombigbee as I pretend every high-pitched "and" coming through my phone is another drop of much-needed rain instead of one more rambling bullet point from my self-involved boss.

"*And* I told Piper she needs to keep better records. I mean, how can I possibly keep up with what I talked about on *Letterman* over, what, *two years ago?*"

"Right."

"So, did you think I looked skinny?"

"Hmm?" I say, stifling a yawn.

"Are you *listening* to me?"

Leaning up to take a sip of organic beer, I can just make out a yellow flicker of light through the hollow from one of the blank window spaces in Joe Tischman's parents' house.

"Phillip? Listen, I don't pay you to *not* listen to me."

"You're not paying me much of anything right now."

"One of my implants is crooked," Frances says.

"Wow. Well. Not what I expected to hear at eleven o'clock at night."

"You can see it. Crooked as hell."

"I'm sorry to hear that. Would these be new implants?"

"Yes. God, you've been gone so long I've already been through another set."

How long have I been gone, a month? No, wait, six?

All I can think of is how badly I wanna jump in the pool and wash off every ounce of juju from this batshit narcissist. "Is this normal?"

"My surgeon says it's not. But sometimes he says it's like when you get a crown on your tooth, you have to go back in to get it adjusted."

"He doesn't sound like a very good surgeon."

"Oh, God, why did you say that? Now you've got me worried."

"I just mean, comparing breasts to teeth? That's not—"

"Oh, who asked you?"

"I gotta go, Frances. I'm sorry about your—things. I'll call you later."

I press the End button and close the phone, an act of rebellion that makes my heart stop cold for a moment. Shaking off the residue of Frances's late night panic, I toss my phone on the concrete and fall face forward into the warm, dark water.

I'd always found comfort in the fact that rattlesnakes sleep at night, especially since I climbed out my bedroom window more than a few times as a kid to traverse the creek banks without so much as a thought to what might lay under my feet. But presently I am recalling an Animal Planet special I'd stumbled across one sleepless night in L.A. that proved, via night vision camerawork, that darkness was their favorite time to move about and hunt. My second beer had given me a strong dose of curiosity, not to mention the courage to move about myself in the surrounding woods. I had to agree with the rattlesnakes. What better time to gather information than in darkness?

Walking cautiously through the bottom of the pitch-black hollow and across the grounds at the back of the Tischman house, I put my hand in front of my face to see if I can see it. For a moment, I can't. Moving past the dark, lifeless tent near the tiny patch of creek beach, I take another sip of beer before climbing the sloping lawn to the rear of the site.

An electric lantern hangs from the ceiling of one of the upstairs rooms. Sizing up the giant aluminum ladder positioned to the left of the window space, I take another sip of liquid courage and begin to climb. I realize how crazy it is and how buzzed I am as soon as I start up.

Peering from below the ledge into what appears to be the skeleton of the master bedroom, I can just make out Joe's bare feet suspended from the area between the downstairs ceiling and the upstairs floor. As his unseen hand hammers loudly on some second-floor surface, his dangling, muscular legs keep his balance, matching every blow from above with a pigeon-toed thrust.

Taking another sip of beer, I attempt to ignore the irritating buzz of a mosquito's wings rising in pitch like a dentist's drill in my ear. Joe's hammering stops for a moment, and I'm almost positive I can hear him sob. One quick outburst of grief before the hammering resumes, but the blows come even faster this time. Grabbing the ladder with the same hand my beer is in, I take a swat at the skeeter with my free hand.

I feel my footing give way a split second before it does. The rung of the ladder sings out a dull, tinny *ping* as I fall, ass over tit, into the pittosporum bushes below.

Even though it was a drop from only three measly rungs, what feels like a good-sized oyster shell lodged in the small of my back tells me not to move. The sound of Joe's feet landing with a thud stops my heart dead. I hear him scuttle across the wooden terrace beside me, and I am suddenly overcome with the smell of myself, soaked to the skin in Jake's Hearty Farms Micro

Beer. From the corner of my eye, I can see Joe's shadow as he stops in the doorless rear entrance of the house.

"Shit," he says, diving out of the house like a paratrooper. He kneels next to me and sets the lantern down by my head. This is going to be worse than I thought. "Are you okay?"

A shrill wheeze whistles from some place in my lungs that brings to mind my father rocking me on the edge of the tub during a bout with the croup.

Joe looks up at the skewed ladder. "Can you breathe?"

I cough. Joe sits back on his haunches, watching me closely with raised eyebrows. He nods and I nod back.

"How we doin'?"

I nod again. "I'm..."

"I've got some things in the tent."

"What? No, I just—"

Joe holds up a hand. "I got some stuff, you'll be fine. Just stay put." He hops up and goes down to the tent. I pull my hands up behind my head to open up my chest, pondering all the awkwardness that comes with allowing yourself to be nurtured, even for the briefest time. A quick gust of summer wind pushes a bat trolling for bugs off its erratic course over the creek below. The cicadas in the surrounding pines take a big collective breath before jumping into their creekside hymn once again, like an animated bug conductor waved his wand from a nearby stump.

"Can I ask you what the hell you were doing?" Joe has already returned from the tent, arms filled with pillows and blankets.

My ears grow fiery hot. "What?"

Joe situates a pillow behind my head and a blanket over my body. "The ladder."

"I was just—I thought I would—I heard you working—" I say, praying for him to interrupt me before I try again. Unable to come up with any respectable pretense, I stifle a nervous laugh. Behind Joe's shoulder, the biggest full moon one is never able to see from foggy Santa Monica has risen over the outline of the house. "Wow," I say at the moon, hoping the looming orb will take some of the focus off me. Joe twists around, studying it. He looks back at me, brushes off his hands, and takes a seat in the grass nearby.

"I need to go," I say, coming to my wobbly knees before a wheeze sits me down again.

"Okay, brother?" he says.

I nod, pulling the blanket over me like a squirmy toddler.

Joe whispers something I can't make out and lies down. He carefully positions a tiny foam pillow underneath his head, watching the sky for a moment before closing his eyes and exhaling a low, tentative groan like a dog somebody let in on a cold, damp night.

He would be in the same position when I went home quietly at dawn.

17

"This is fucking scary," Sis reports from the back seat of the pickup. I had cajoled Garrett into letting me borrow his newest, a crimson Ford F-150, by claiming I needed to help Patience move some furniture. A pickup, even a brand-new one, would blend in far more easily with the dodgy surroundings than Tina's Lincoln.

"It is what it is," Patience tells Sis from the passenger seat next to me, checking a map in her lap and eyeballing the dirty, diminutive house situated literally across the railroad tracks.

The last time I patronized this so-called place of business, I was a senior in high school taking a bet I could make the long walk unaccompanied from Patience's car door to the open service window around back. There, a hostile African American girl would sell you a nickel bag of inferior weed, but only after an older man, a paraplegic who looked just like Morgan Freeman, gave her the okay from his daybed.

Tracing my steps twenty years later, the most I can cough up as the Bahama window is punched open is, "Hi. Um. I need."

The girl, now a cruelly overweight woman with cavernous creases in her face, studies my partners in crime behind me. Patience smiles and nods in encouragement while Sis pops her gum, digging in her ear with her free hand.

"You police?" the woman says.

The door behind the woman blasts open as the old man, lying sideways on a gurney, pulls himself through the door and down the wall like a spider. "You a narc?" he says.

Spotting the barrel of a sawed-off shotgun protruding from under his housecoat, I move back a step. "No. We're just..." I glance back at Patience, who winks from some blond Zen state I've never been privy to. Turning back to the window, I smile like someone running for office. I lean on the windowsill, knowing I'm taking my life in my own hands. "I need some hash. Not a lot, like a dime bag, maybe?" I turn to Patience, who nudges me along with a raised eyebrow. "It's for baking."

"Baking?" the woman asks incredulously. She turns to the old man, who offers up a half laugh. "Dime bag?"

"I don't think they have those anymore," Sis whispers, "so why don't you hop into the twentieth century before you get us all killed." I look to Patience, who shrugs, mumbling something about inflation.

"Oh," I say. "Well, whatever—wherever—you start. On the hash. Hish."

The woman turns to the old man, who gives her the nod. As if out of thin air, the woman drops a tiny brown paper bag on the shelf on her side of the sill. "One hundred."

"One hundred," I say obediently, like a first grade spelling student.

"ONE HUNDRED!" she screams. The old man watches me close, steadying himself on the squeaky gurney.

I turn to Sis. "I've only got sixty-five."

She rolls her eyes. "My purse is in the truck."

❖

Perusing *The Macrobiotic Way*, the recipe for Adzuki Bean Brownies would have screamed inedible in every way possible.

But, oddly enough, the addition of one special ingredient took the dish to a whole other dimension. Especially on a third serving.

"These are *really* good." Tina's front teeth are blacked out by the goopy treats, a sight she would find objectionable. "I don't even *feel* like I've had chemo. It's more like…it's more like…" She reclines farther back on the king-sized bed, watching the fingers of her right hand dance a playful jig above her head. "I want another one."

Taking the knife from the cake plate between us, I cut one of the delectables in half. "I tell you what, I'll split one with you."

Tina sits up, glancing at a snoring Sis on the floor next to the bathroom door. "Shh, don't wake the sleeping bear," she says, giggling and clapping her hands once before she stops herself. She licks some brownie off her fingers and giggles some more.

"What the hell is this?"

Tina and I sit up straight as we can at Garrett's intrusion. Holding the baggie above his head, he waits for an answer like he's Moses just back with the tablets.

Tina points at me through another blacked-out smile. "He made brownies." She kicks me in the side, and I lay the knife back down on the plate, trying not to laugh.

"Are you all high on dope?" he says to me and no one else.

Tina is suddenly serious. "*I* am." She points to me. "He's not."

Garrett pitches the bag on the chest of drawers. "Bo Skeet, can I see you for a moment?"

"What's the matter? Of course you can see me. You're seeing me right here!" I say, concerned I might pee the bed.

Garrett is unmoved. "I *said* now. And now means now."

The fact that Garrett has interrupted the first pot buzz I've had since college tempts me to ignore him and the pall he's brought to the proceedings. Setting the cake plate aside, I make a valiant attempt to haul myself off the bed, stepping over a still-sleeping Sis until I come face-to-face with his gaze of judgment.

Tina hollers groggily. "Gaaaaaarrett. You have a halo aaaaaall around your head."

Garrett rolls his eyes and walks away.

"You're high, too." Tina giggles.

❖

Garrett leans against the support pilaster on the front porch, looking out over Blue Cove Road like a watchtower fireman. I stay close to the door, attempting to conceal the brownie half I'm still holding in my left hand. "Is that Marv Tischman's boy I saw doing that work on his mama and daddy's house?"

"Yeah," I say, realizing my paltry answer sounds more like a question than a statement.

"Well, that's about as near-a-next-to-nothing as you're gonna get."

Garrett has used this phrase every since I can remember, always in reference to the worst of its lot. "Why do you say that?"

Garrett makes a face that doesn't answer my question.

I go again, but I suspect it's a bad idea. "What does the face mean?"

"Listen, I don't know what you're trying to pull here."

My debilitating case of cottonmouth has more to do with Joe than it does with the dope. I know Garrett saw us talking the other day, but surely he has no idea I spent last night there. Or that the reason I had to was because I wasn't minding my own business. "What are you talking about?"

"What you're doin' in my house is illegal."

I am more than a bit relieved we're leaving the subject of Joe and getting back to the felony at hand.

"Doctors write prescriptions for this stuff out in California all the time," I say.

Garrett rolls his eyes at the mere mention of the freewheeling state. "Well, I don't doubt that. Now, I haven't said a word about any of this tofu crap, but I'm drawing the line right here. You got me?" He folds his arms across his chest like he's the Chief of Everything.

I'll get anything he wants me to if I can just get a glass of water down my rusty pipes. "I got you. Just don't—"

Garrett raises a threatening eyebrow.

"I got you," I say again, ducking back into the house.

18

The Tischman house has seen substantial growth since I was last here, its exposed frames and open lofts replaced with walls and doors, giving the place an impenetrable air. The past several weeks have been jam-packed between doctor visits, shopping, and the preparation of three macrobiotic meals a day. For the first time in ages, I'm asleep most nights before eleven.

Having finally gotten the whole thing down to a science, I've decided to broaden my horizons and head back to the scene of the crime. A crime I've relived many times during my rare free time. Although the incident left me too bruised to brave any further embarrassment with another visit, I've decided to throw caution to the wind.

I can make out Joe's lopsided smile in the late afternoon sun all the way from the creek trail. I allow myself a few extra seconds of unnecessary maneuvering amidst the brush and brambles to soak in that feeling of anticipation one carries, light as a feather, on their way to meet someone who has caught their attention. Joe sips a bottle of beer in a wrought iron patio chair and squints curiously as I advance the steps.

"I thought I was going to have to send a messenger," he says.

"And what would said messenger have said?"

Joe smiles, waving goodbye to a pair of weary-looking

Latino carpenters lobbing their toolboxes into an old pickup truck in the driveway. "How 'bout some contraband?" he says, holding up his near-empty beer. "Well, guess I can't call it that anymore, can I?"

"Nah, you can't. And I'm good, but thanks." I truly am, feeling now more than ever the Gospel According to Justin and Marsala. My body is humming from an early dinner of millet and seitan, while my mind buzzes with limitless possibilities. It suddenly dawns on me Joe's tent was no longer pitched under the chinaberry. "Where's your tent?" I say, swatting a no-see-um, wondering if the bug is any relation to the pest that got me into this situation in the first place.

"We got walls now. I moved in," he says, pointing his thumb over his shoulder at the house. "How 'bout a beer and that tour?"

"What?"

Joe ambles into my personal space. "You seem nervous."

Wow. Am I about to meet the crazy Sis talked about? "Who, me? Nervous? No, I'm not nervous. Why should I be?"

"There's something on your neck," he says, squinting just above my collar. "Some flying something."

"What? Get it before it bites. Everything down here bites."

"All right," he says, placing a hand aside my neck. "I'm lying. I just wanted an excuse to touch you, but I didn't want to wait for a perfect moment in the conversation. So. I'm just gonna leave my hand here for a while."

I can feel my heart beat in my neck underneath his big sweaty hand. I can look everywhere but in his eyes, which is a shame as that's probably the only place I should be looking, just in case he *is* nuts. But he doesn't feel nuts. It feels like he's trying to soothe the heartbeat in my neck with his cool, calm energy. I suddenly feel scared and sleepy at the same time.

"So. Since you haven't coldcocked me yet, does that mean I can kiss you?"

"You..." I say, only now beginning to wrap my head around what's actually about to happen.

"Otherwise I'm gonna look like an idiot with some dumb-ass bug ruse."

"Well, I haven't coldcocked anyone in a mighty long time. I usually try and keep my violently short temper in check."

Joe kisses me once, quick. I'm thinking maybe it's too quick, but he comes in for another. This time he stays a couple seconds longer. The top of my scalp is tingling. As he pulls away, he smiles the tiniest of smiles, moves his hand to the side of my face, and pats it gently.

Stuffing my hands in my pockets, I take in the Tischman house behind us, trying to think of something to say.

"How 'bout that tour?" Joe says, tilting his head back as if to get a better look at me.

"How 'bout that beer?" I'm stalling what I feel sure is inevitable.

"Is that a beer *and* a tour, or a beer *instead* of the tour?"

Abruptly robbed of all pretenses, I take a seat, if only for a moment, in Joe's vacant chair.

❖

"So, wait," he says. "You've never kissed a guy on the lips?"

"Nope. And it's not the stereotype from pulp novels where the straight guy says, 'We can do everything else, but I don't kiss.' I've been with guys—well, a couple, and just briefly."

"But no kissing."

"Crazy, I guess. I've just never thought about it before." I give Joe's waist a tug. "So what does it feel like to have not an ounce of fat on your body?"

Joe doesn't answer. He plays with a lock of sweaty hair on my forehead.

I'm thinking how insane it is to realize I've never lain side by side facing a girl the way I'm presently lying with Joe. This in and of itself, I suppose, means nothing. I've collapsed above and below a lover, spooned, even chatted head to toe and toe to head. It's just a simple observation. In a sea of blankets tossed about a futon on this sawdust-covered floor, the fact that Joe's leg is thrown over mine in a most familiar way is making an indelible impression. It's definitely a day of firsts. "Personally," I say, "I've been able to pinch way more than an inch since I discovered beer in college."

"You're fine."

"You're a nice guy for saying so."

"Now, that's true. I *am* a nice guy," he says as a mockingbird trills enthusiastically outside the bedroom window. "Isn't that something?" Joe tilts his head up toward the window where the mockingbird is aping a jenny wren like a champ. "How a mocker can do that? I mean, how does he even know to try and take on someone else's song? I heard one mock a cat once. About dusk one day. Scared me half to death."

"Do you know that until I was about thirty years old, I didn't know that mockingbirds actually *mocked* other birds?"

"What? No."

"I was out in the boat one day with Garrett, and he said, 'Listen at that bird mocking a robin' and I was like, 'What are you *talking* about?'"

Joe's shoulders rise and fall with laughter under the blanket as he takes in the ridiculous confession. "So, why did you think they called them mockingbirds?"

"I'd never really thought about it. I just thought they had a rich and varied playlist," I say, cackling, my face red with embarrassment.

Joe presses his erection against my calf. "You are one crazy *shaigitz*."

I press back with my leg even harder, like it's a contest.

"What was it like to be the only Jewish kid in town?"

"Was I?" he says, a fake look of shock on his face.

"You were. And I remember thinking it was so cool. But some of the old people at church thought you were going to hell."

"I think because my father wasn't made it okay with some

of 'em. And we had a tree at Christmas. But the menorah thing, and the fact that we didn't go to *any* church was unacceptable."

"One of our gurus in Tennessee is Jewish," I say, sounding alarmingly like my mother.

"Gurus?"

"Story for another day. Where'd 'Irondick' come from?"

"I have no idea."

I give him a look that says I don't believe him.

"I'm a hundred percent serious."

"Well," I say, feeling around under the covers. "A very reliable source tells me you came by it honest."

"Oh, and who is that?"

"Me," I say, pulling his cock forward and letting it slap back hard on his stomach. "But I have to do more research."

"You won't *do*, boy," Joe says.

"How'd you come to building houses?" I love the fact that when two people are together, they can do one thing and talk about another.

Joe scratches my lower back lightly with his fingernails, an action that causes every hair on my body to stand at full mast. "Spent a summer with Habitat for Humanity. Got hooked. Then I decided to find out how the other half lived—you know, the folks who live and die thinking only of themselves."

"And how's that working out for you?" I say, wondering if I should be doing something to him to make his body feel as good as mine does.

"I love it. I'm trying to live as selfishly as I possibly can for as long as I can possibly stand it."

I find myself wondering if this is when he's going to add they had to bring him home in a straightjacket. Quite honestly, I can't pick up one speck of nervous in this guy's staunch demeanor. My heart double-times, that place where you nod off and wake yourself in the same split second. "Go to sleep. We don't have to talk," he says softly.

"No, I just...what was India like?"

"Beautiful. Dirty. Crowded. Amazing. Every fantastic and terrible thing you've heard about India is true, to the tenth power." He moves his chin to my shoulder. "Hey. You want a drink? A beer, water or—hey," he says, looking back over his shoulder, "what are you doing back there?"

"Aren't there supposed to be, like, thirty-two vertebrae?" I say, my lips softly calculating as I move my hand slowly down the middle of his back.

"I guess." Joe stays perfectly still, closing his eyes, a hint of smile crossing his leathery, sunburned face.

I continue to tally, quiet, intense. "Wow, they go so far down," I say, playing the upper ones like some crazy xylophone with my other hand.

Joe giggles and flinches. "Do they?"

"Am I tickling you?"

"Sort of. It's okay," he says, putting both arms around the top of my shoulders, pulling the leg that's already over mine in tighter. "Is that better?"

"Yep," I say, pulling him even closer. "Yep."

❖

RRRRRRRRRRRoooooooooowwwwwwwww. The piercing wail of a troubled cat calls from somewhere in the distance as I snake down the creek trail, briefly catching the silhouette of my father standing under one of the water oaks at the top of the hollow.

RRRRRRRRooooooooowww. The cat sounds worse for wear as I squat next to the creek, covertly tossing water on my face and under my arms, a poor attempt to generate nonexistent jogger's sweat.

"You must have gotten off early this morning," he says, squatting to tie his shoe.

Pulling the cap down over my forehead, I attempt to ignore my father's unintentional double entendre while I conceal my face.

"You check any o' them crawfish traps?" Garrett asks.

"Yeah," I say, referring to the tiny boxes he rigs on the creek beds to catch the mudbugs he uses for bait. "Not a lot going on." Louisiana may hold the crown for quantity, but Alabama has more species of crawfish than any other state. Bass love to see them squirming on the end of a hook.

"What, couldn't sleep?"

"Nope," I say, attempting to make my way past him, as if he can read my mind like a sideshow psychic.

RRRRRRRRRRRRROoooooooooooooowwwwwww. It seems highly probable this yowl could be the anguished mystery cat's final call.

"What the devil..." I say.

"You gotta see this thing," Garrett says, heading toward the swimming pool. "Come on."

I follow my father into the sunlight where he produces a remote control from his pocket. He aims it at a black cube the size of a shoebox near the carport. "You know all the trouble we've been having with crows?" he says.

"What trouble?" I wasn't aware crows caused strife of any kind.

"Well, you know," Garrett says, screwing up his face, "a crow's just a crow."

RRRRRRRROoooooooooowwwwwwww.

"This is a predator call," he says, pointing the remote at the box and flipping a switch, excited as a kid at Christmas. "Now, see, this is a house cat in distress. And when that crow hears that house cat, he's gonna come a' flyin'. And I'm gonna be waiting for him with my .22 rifle. No, wait," he says, pulling the instructions out of his pocket, scanning them. "The *coyotes* are gonna come for the distressed house cat."

"What coyotes?"

Another click, this time a *cock-a-doodle-do*.

"What's that?" I ask.

"That would be," Garrett says, reading, "the pleading chicken. And that attracts—lemme see—that attracts the coyotes, as well."

"Gonna be a pretty tough day around here for coyotes."

Baaaaaahhhh.

"Let me guess," I say, "pleading sheep?"

"Bleating billy goat."

"Attracts?"

"General predators. Gray foxes, barn owl, what have you."

The lunacy of my father and I actually having such a lively, illuminating conversation about a subject of such grisliness strikes me as peculiar.

"What else you got?" I ask, feeling less and less than ever like the shamed nine-year-old who pulled the trigger on the turkey gobbler.

BBBBBBwwwwwwwwwwaaaaaaahhh. Something between a shriek and a squawk.

Garrett grins from ear to ear. "Whining baby cottontail. Probably caught on a fence or something and can't get out."

I make a face and ask for another, my eagerness to continue the discourse overriding the guilt I feel in this twisted game of Darwinism.

Squeeeeeeaaaaaaakkkkkkk.

"Distressed rodent?"

"Field mouse!" my father says, nodding. "And what predator would we be calling?"

"Ah, hawk?"

"A hawk would go ape shit for a field mouse," he says, pleased as punch.

I pull my pants up tight around my waist and ask for another.

THE DIXIE

October 28, 1999
Headlines

Alcohol Sales Begin in Jackson

The first beer and wine in Jackson's history has now been sold at three area stores. For some who led the attempt to keep the city free from alcoholic sales, like the Rev. C.C. Tompkins, it was not a time of celebration. "As a pastor, I think it is now time for our churches to begin to set our sights on ministering to folks that are going to be affected by the inflow of alcohol." Those who felt differently, like Walker Springs Grab and Go (now Walker Springs Beer Barn) owner Kristy Kelp, cheerfully heralded a new day for businesses. "First weekend sales have been unbelievable. I've hardly even had time to sit down and smoke," Kelp said. "I think things will settle down in a few weeks, but I think you can see that the people are definitely going to come to Jackson now that we have beer for sale."

19

Billy Wade is driving on an untamed country highway during that unpredictable time of day when the last blip of sunset is giving itself over to darkness. Patience sips a beer and navigates next to him. In the back seat, Joe slides his big right foot up next to the side of my left one while I'm wrestling with reception on my cell.

"I don't *know* when I'll be back…Frances, listen…I know it *seems* there's no way you can make it without me, but—"

Billy Wade snorts from behind the wheel of the cement truck. "Oh, brother."

"Selfish!" Patience hollers.

I hush both of them with a cold stink eye, and Patience points at a road sign. "Mile seventeen marker!"

"Shh!" I hiss to no avail as Joe puts his hand over mine. In the rearview mirror, I can see Patience pretend she didn't see it as I gently push his hand away.

Billy Wade swerves down a distant kin of drivable road. "THIS IS IT!"

"I gotta go, Frances. Visitors' hours are almost over." I toss the cell on the seat next to me. "So," I say to my fellow trekkers, "do I get to know where we're going?"

Patience bounces like a toddler. "It's a surprise!" she says, turning around and flinging a Cheshire grin at me, then at Joe, then at me again, her happiness in being in on the secret more than she can bear. I stare back, chewing my lip, something she always said I did whenever she was pissing me off. She takes another pull off her beer and flings the bottle out the window at a yield sign on the side of the road. The glass shatters, and she and Billy Wade whoop.

"I can't believe you did that," I say.

"Ha ha! Two points!" she says with a wink at Joe before focusing again on me. "Okay, remember Jimbo Pritchett?"

Billy Wade waves Patience down with a wild arm. "Shush!"

"The Piggly Wiggly Easter Bunny?" I say, pushing Billy Wade's arm back into his own territory.

"Yessiree."

I turn to Billy Wade, hoping he's giving me more.

"Let's just say," Patience says, choosing her words gingerly, "the biggest stars are not *always* found in Hollyweird."

"Oh, shit," Billy Wade says, pulling the car to the side of the road with a skid as a hay truck passes in the other lane.

"Hay truck, bow your head, make a wish!" Patience hollers.

"Bow your head!" Joe hollers at me through a half-serious grin, tucking his head behind the seat.

"What are you wishing for?" I ask Joe, bowing my head.

Joe lowers his voice. "That when we get home, you'll try that thing you *wouldn't* try the other night."

"I heard that," Patience says.

Genuinely embarrassed, I lower my head even more, giggling like a hyena.

Once we've avoided the wrath of the hay truck's curse, Billy Wade pulls back into the highway before he quickly makes a left turn, maneuvering the vehicle through a rocky stream and up a narrow, washed-out hill. "Hold on to whatcha got."

❖

Our motley crew joins a group of twenty-five others outside a crumbling turquoise house trailer. Ancient aluminum lawn chairs have been assembled in the muddy yard, a sort of audience directed at the tiny front porch. Billy Wade pushes me down into an aisle seat next to Joe. Patience motions Billy Wade to sit next to her in one of the shortie beach chairs down front.

A nervous, buttoned-down business type across the aisle from me avoids eye contact with anyone, while one of a pair of would-be female sumo wrestlers seated next to Joe whispers, "First time here?"

The crowd begins to quiet in anticipation as someone turns down the camp lantern hanging from a nearby cypress tree. An announcement, an English woman's voice through a cheap sound system, opens the dubious proceedings. "Ladies and gentlemen, the management would like to remind you that the use of cameras, recording devices, and cell phones are strictly prohibited in the amphitheater. And now it is our great pleasure to once again ask you to put your hands together and give a warm Gulf Coast welcome to the incomparable—the irrepressible—Miss—JEANNIE LEE WAGNER!"

A mechanic's shop light positioned over the porch flicks on as someone resembling a chunky dime store version of Elizabeth Taylor exits the front door of the trailer. Jimbo Pritchett, aka Jeannie Lee, twists and gyrates to the first few bars of a country tune I've never heard like he's playing the main room at the Sands. Pulling seductively at the hem of his mini, he adjusts the back of his wig with a tug, tracing the side of his face with a white-gloved hand as he begins to lip-sync over the fans' wild applause.

Billy Wade and Patience turn around to check my reaction. Still attempting to find my footing in this *Deliverance*-tinged wonderland, I whisper, "Jimbo Pritchett is a drag queen?"

Billy Wade snorts. "First Friday of the month here. And every other Saturday at the Foxx Club in Mobile."

I look up to find Jimbo's eyes locked on mine, and he's prancing my way. I pray that if I look straight ahead with enough steel cold horror in my eyes, he'll look somewhere else. Or choke on a chicken bone. Anything.

And just like that, I have a two-hundred-pound drag queen sitting on my lap. Jimbo pulls a giant feathered boa around my neck and breaks his tune to address the audience. Trying to go inside myself to see if I can will my own death, I think I hear him say, "Ladies and gentlemen, we've got a *celebrity* in the audience tonight."

Uh-oh, here it comes.

"Miss Frances Newman's boy toy, Phillip Stalworth. All the way from Hooooollywood!"

Everyone whoops and hollers, even Business Type. The sumo wrestlers next to us hold up their beer cans, crashing them into other beer cans around them.

Holding up my own beer, I take a healthy slug before toasting Joe and everyone else around me. Jimbo pats me gently on the back, and I belch like a sweetly rocked baby.

❖

The gentle heat from Jimbo's primitive fridge is finally beginning to dry the night mist saturating my sweatshirt from an hour-and-a-half show and two curtain calls. Nursing a plastic cup of wine I retrieved from a box on the trailer steps, I'm doing my best to avoid one more question about my famous pedigree while Billy Wade, Patience, and Joe cut a tiny space of rug in Jimbo's living room. I make my way discreetly past a wall of country music collector plates to a card table bearing Hydrox, chips, and California dip.

"Stay on the plywood, the rest is rotten." Jimbo, still in drag, points to the planks of plywood on the floor in a husky voice. "Don't wanna lose any Hollywood royalty."

"Oh. Right," I say, eyeballing the decking beneath our feet with suspicion.

Jimbo offers up a plate of dubious delights from the back of the table. "Have one—it's the *good* Cheez Whiz." Jimbo takes off his wig and glances at Joe, who's dancing like a high school principal, his stiff arms resting on top of his head. "Joe Tischman's still hot as hell. You think he'd go out with me?"

I take a healthy slug of my beer, noticing Joe has one shoe on and one shoe off. "Prob'ly."

20

In the South, folks have told stories from their front porches for eons, most of them tall. And more often than not, they will end the tale with, "I kid you not, *this* is a true story!" Now, I don't know if it's the heat, the religion, our history of hysteria, *or* our hysterical history, but the place breeds peculiar natives. With this many peculiar people on one land mass, peculiar happenings are just part of the landscape. "*This*—is a true story." This just means, if you're a Yankee, and you think what I've just told you couldn't possibly have happened, then think again. 'Cause this shit might not happen in Bangor, Maine, but you can bet your sweet *ass* it happens here.

There is a brand of mind control called the Silva Method that's been around since the sixties. Developed by a pseudoscientist from Europe, it entails whipping yourself into a state of alpha where, through creative visualization, you can accomplish anything: write the Great American Novel, climb the corporate ladder, heal your body from disease or—my favorite—heal someone *else's* body for them. You can imagine my enthusiasm when I saw there would be a class taught in Mobile, an hour away.

It's really very simple: One sits on the edge of his or her bed every morning upon rising. This is where the magic happens. The first week is preparation. One starts the day by counting backward from fifty—slowly—in complete and utter silence. That's it. For the first week.

But *then*…you pick what you want to do—and you picture it—eyes closed. This puts you in alpha. For the second week.

Then, as soon as you feel comfortable, you tilt your head up, keeping your visual intact, but your eyes closed. Tina and I were told that this initially makes most people feel light-headed, like someone kicked the feet out from under them. And it was no different for us.

So pay attention, 'cause now you're ready for the big guns: TRANSFER YOUR VISION TO THE LEFT.

So. That's:

    a.   Close your eyes
    b.   Visualize something
    c.   Move it up
    d.   Then move it to the left

This is where things get a little dicey, and frankly, from a storytelling point of view, I have no yardstick to measure any of it against. So this is exactly what happened:

I was hoping to get the morning paper before Puffy got up and off her stoop. Instead, I find her standing on the grass below our front porch steps, top lip aquiver. "Hello, Puffy," I say, kneeling slowly to pick up the weekly edition of *The Dixie*. "You ugly little motherfucker."

"HEEEEERE, PUFFY-PUFFY-PUFFY!" Jewel Ann hollers, making a beeline for me and the miserable little Yorkie before I turn quickly and head back up the steps like my pants are on fire. "Phil!" Jewel Ann shrieks and I grudgingly turn around, bracing myself for another acid reflux anecdote. "What was the counting this morning?"

I pull my robe close around me to prevent any awkward surprise appearances. "Huh?"

Jewel Ann scoops up Puffy, checking the pooch's ragged little nails. "I heard counting this morning. Sounded like counting—coming from this direction. A man, best I could tell. Loud, no voice I knew. Sounded like somebody counting backward. Did you hear it?"

Since Tina and I were the only two who took the class and, so far, hadn't shared any of the details with Joe nor anyone else, I wasn't quite sure how to respond. Since the two of us would have been counting in silence, as instructed, all I could offer Jewel Ann was a weak "Hu-uh" before going back inside.

Later, while reporting the story to the other members of my family, there was no explanation. No one seemed particularly spooked by the tale. It was just this creepy, crazy story that I'm sure in my later years will disappear completely from my radar. But I hope like hell it doesn't.

21

The grandfather clock gongs midnight, eliciting a tiny jerk from my wobbly body as I creep down the hallway to my bedroom, having seen Joe for a second time today. Making a mental note to remember to tell Garrett to oil my squeaky bathroom door, I brush my teeth and fall into bed.

Waiting on my bedside table are the last few chapters of a memoir written by a Philadelphia physician who, upon receiving the news of his inoperable cancer, went on macrobiotics and lived well for seven years before trading it briefly for a diet of red meat and cheese while touring Europe. Within two months, he was dead.

At three a.m., I finally turn out the light, the musk of Joe's aftershave clinging faintly to the T-shirt I've decided to sleep in for that very reason. Instantaneously reanimated, I make another mental note to pass the book on to Tina, with strict instructions to finish it *tout de suite.*

Plumping the down pillow, I roll on my stomach, recalling Joe's amusement when he told me that, during the peak of passion, I said a word he swore sounded just like *koirnk!* Having no recollection of this moment or that word, I good-naturedly called him a lying sack and vowed to never again make any sound whatsoever in his presence. I kept my vow until he retrieved an imaginary dictionary from underneath the futon, reading aloud the definition of koirnk: "a really good word used by only the most extraordinary of Southern gentlemen indicating, more frequently than not, zeal, fervor, and enthusiasm."

Right after this exchange, Joe reminded me it had already been nine months since we met, or re-met. Nine months since I had tossed my useless life in the toilet and returned to a place where I'd presumed I had nothing. I had done my best to conceal how touched I was he was keeping track.

Taking another whiff of the shirt, I reach over and, feeling for the diet book, toss it on the floor so I'll bump into it in the morning on the way to my day.

❖

Having uncharacteristically overslept, I had been forced to postpone my run, instead heading directly into breakfast preparations. A few hours later, the Gulf Coast breeze keeps me relatively cool as I finally complete my jog, entering the house to the unmistakable aroma of Sunday dinners past. No meal is as important as Sunday dinner, the highly anticipated repast rewarding those who have endured their fair share of hellfire and brimstone.

As I make my way toward the kitchen while fanning my sticky shirt in the welcoming frost of the air-conditioning, Garrett calls from where he stands at the bar, pulling bucket after bucket of Colonel Sanders from four large white paper bags.

"Hey, Bo Skeet, how was the jog?" he says.

"Excuse me," I say, momentarily checking the lunacy-tracking device in my head, "but what are you doing?"

"I got dinner," he says with a big grin. "To celebrate. Sis just sold two houses, so she's gonna be staying with us for a couple of weeks. You know, change of scenery."

My feet are cemented to the bright yellow tile like bridge pilings. "You…"

He brandishes a stack of Chinette he takes from a grocery bag. "See? I even got plates."

"You're kidding me, right?" I say, offering him one last chance to get on the train.

"I just thought for one day, we'd have a change. Um," he says, snatching a drumstick from one of the buckets, tearing into it while he continues unpacking. He dangles it in front of my face. "Extra crispy."

"I don't—this is—" I sputter, turning around, searching for the macrobiotic book of horrors I'd brought downstairs with me. I toss Garrett a menacing look over my shoulder before I find the memoir on a living room end table, holding it next to my face as first and only evidence. "Do you want *this* to happen to Tina?" I ask, my eyeballs bulging like a thyroidal Pekingese.

Garrett rolls his eyes and brings two buckets to the breakfast table. "It's just one meal."

I point sharply at the book, taking two big steps closer to my father. "That's what he said. And now he's dead."

Sis enters from the patio, tossing her backpack on one of the breakfast room table chairs. "Oh, my God, *chicken!*" she says to Garrett, tilting her head in my direction. "Is he gonna let us have this?"

"I'm sure fucking not gonna"—I say, whispering so that Tina, wherever she is, won't overhear—"let us have it!" Grabbing the bags, buckets, and half-eaten chicken legs in one fell swoop like a selfish toddler, I open the patio door with two free fingers and head to the garbage cans.

"That's thirty dollars' worth of chicken!" Garrett yells out the door.

"I want you both out of the kitchen," I say. "I'm going to prepare a special treat, something I had already planned for Sunday dinner if you had just given me the chance." I drop the buckets and slam the lid on the can. "Tina deserves our support. It's the least we could do to keep any fast food aromas off the premises." I take two steps behind one of the receptacles in case someone decides to throw something.

Sis mumbles to Garrett. "Probably mung beans and boiled crap. No, crap would be considered flesh," she says, pleased with her stinging, nonsensical aside.

"Just go," I say, moving a bit farther behind one of the cans. "I'll call you when it's ready."

Tina, her hair still wet from a late morning shower, enters the kitchen and sniffs the leftover chicken air. "Yuuum," she says, "when *what's* ready?"

❖

You haven't lived until you've been to the grand opening of a Walmart in a town of four thousand people. It's like somebody dropped New York City smack dab in the middle of Mayberry. The town is a frenzy. My father is beside himself.

"Y'all better be gettin' down to that Walmart. Why, somebody said they got all kinds of exotic fruits and vegetables the likes of which this town, or any other town, ain't never seen."

I wondered if Walmart could be the answer to our natural living prayers since our dimwitted friend at Healthy Way Foods wasn't yet set up for produce. I was one of the first to line up at the door, third only to Percy Janks, a prehistoric postman from Walker Springs, and Cal Hunt, a former classmate of mine who stored the boogers he ate for recess underneath his desk well into eighth grade.

At seven a.m. promptly, I burst through the sliding glass doors past an old lady who yodeled, "Welcome to Walmart," as she jammed a sale paper into my side.

"The produce," I say, "fresh produce." She points. I speed past the scores of pop culture junk and stop, frozen, unfazed that "O Little Town of Bethlehem" is coming through the PA system with two months left of spring. Directly in front of me is the most beautiful sight I have ever seen. Throngs of crisp, freshly picked vegetables—bok choy, daikon radish, lotus root—the staples of macrobiotic cooking. I begin to pick as if from the Tree of Life itself. I pick and pick, and then I pick some more. I want it all, just in case it was only for opening day show, so they'll be sure to order more. I picture a sepia-toned scene, the Walmart manager dressed in a bolo tie and butcher's apron, frantically calling through the mouthpiece of one of those ancient wall phones. "Send more parsnips *immediately.* It's a matter of life and death!"

And it would be.

I gather with the rest of the town on the bright green lawn outside. Mayor Nellie Huff christens the day "A New Age of Shopping in Clarke County," a title more relevant for me than most of my fellow shoppers.

Fingering my bags of produce, I look to the heavens over the LOW PRICE LEADER sign, my heart full of gratitude. "Thank you, Jesus." I positively radiate.

❖

"Looking good!" I kneel next to the swimming pool with a stopwatch in my hand as Tina finishes another lightning-speed lap. Frances buzzes my ear bud with news of dyspeptic producers and reshoots.

"I slept with the director during rehearsals. I didn't fake it, if you know what I mean, so he got upset."

"Did nobody tell you that you don't have to sleep with the director once you have the job?"

"But I think I replaced someone else. I wanted to make sure he was happy with the choice."

"Atta girl."

"I feel twenty years younger," Tina calls as she swims to the edge of the pool.

"Do you think I should get veneers?" Frances asks.

"Frances, I have to go and get my mother her medicine."

"Oh, I'm sorry, all about me. How is your mother? Is she still doing well?"

"No, she's not doing well at all."

Tina gets out and I hand her a towel. "Will you be a dear and spot me on some bench presses?" she says, heading for the basement. "I wanna try out some of those free weights of yours."

"Free weights?" I ask, not sure what I've heard.

"Yes, free weights."

"Are you sure?"

Tina calls out over her shoulder, "Sure, I'm sure!"

I am struck by the overwhelming evidence that our path of doom and destruction has taken a turn of almost biblical proportions.

THE DIXIE

April 17, 2000
Community

Alcohol Regulations Put Into Place

In response to the citizens of Jackson voting to permit the sale of alcohol within the city limits, the City Council is now approving a lengthy ordinance governing the regulation of alcohol beverage sales and distribution. Details of the ordinance will be printed in *The Dixie* as they become available. Those reading the ordinance in its entirety are forewarned that it contains explicit language:

1. It shall be unlawful for any person or their associations to permit the following on any licensed premises:
    a. Topless or bottomless waitresses, waiters, dancers or cashiers.
    b. Acts, or simulated acts, of caressing or fondling of the breasts, buttocks, anus or genitals.
    c. Acts, or simulated acts, of sexual intercourse, masturbation, sodomy, bestiality, oral

copulation, flagellation or any sexual acts which are prohibited by law.

d. Acts involving the displaying of the anus, vulva or genitals.

e. The showing of any visual reproductions depicting scenes wherein artificial devices or inanimate objects are employed to depict any of the prohibited activities described above in this section.

Next week: Open Containers and What They Mean to You

22

Sipping a beer on my parents' pool steps, I lean back on my elbows, taking in the sight of Joe swimming laps like an Olympic champ.

"I forgot how much I love to swim in the dark. When are you coming in?" he says, stopping in front of me to catch his breath.

"Where did you learn to do that?"

"What, the crawl?"

"I always wanted to swim like that."

"But you can swim," he says.

"Of course I can swim, but it's an ugly swim. Nothing special."

"I think you're something special," he says, crawling up a couple of steps and planting his face in the crotch of my swimsuit.

"Whoa. I don't think this is acceptable behavior in the bylaws of the official games."

Joe sticks his face up the leg of my shorts and sniffs.

"What's going on down there?" I say, gasping and laughing as he tickles the inside of my thigh with his tongue.

He pulls back, looks up. "Put down the beer."

"I will in a second. So, when did your folks learn you liked guys?"

"Oh. Well." Joe grabs a beach ball and floats on it. "My mother found a magazine under my bed when she was cleaning.

It was the worst magazine she could have found. Orgies, flying body fluids, you name it."

"So what did she do?"

"She left it on my bed with a pamphlet on AIDS and a box of condoms."

"No way," I say.

"Jewish mothers, you gotta love 'em."

"Indeed."

Joe tosses the ball into the deep end. "So, are you gonna put down the beer now?"

"Yes, sir," I say, taking one last slug.

He shimmies out of his trunks and tosses them on the side of the pool. "Now you."

"You're certainly giving out the instructions this evening." I peel off my trunks. "Anything else I can do for you?"

"Oh, yeah," he says. "Here we go." Grabbing me by the waist, Joe pulls me off the steps into the water. He sits cross-legged on the bottom of the shallow end of the pool and situates me on top of him. He places my hands around the back of his neck. "Do you like me?"

"Of course I like you. Can't you tell?" I say, placing his hand on my cock.

"Well, I know you like me like that," Joe says with a grin. "I mean, who wouldn't?"

Who wouldn't, indeed, I think, laughing out loud.

"Shh. We don't wanna wake your folks."

"Right, no."

"Thank you for inviting me over," Joe says, taking in the surroundings. "I like it back here. Do y'all not have a pool light?"

"It doesn't work."

"Just as well for tonight, I guess. It feels like we're in high school," he says, running his fingernails lightly down my back. "Fooling around in the parents' pool. With beer."

"It does," I say, feeling not a day over sixteen.

"So, I'm gonna ask you again."

"What's that?"

Joe whispers softly in my ear. "Do you like me?"

"We've already covered this."

"Not like *that*," he says, resting his head on my shoulder like a child.

The vulnerability in his voice startles me. It takes me a moment to find my bearings. I can hear the water gurgling through the skimmer behind us. "I like you," I whisper.

After a moment, Joe pulls away from me and looks into my eyes with a face of relief and contentment. It's such a switch from the sexy, gregarious man I've come to know, it brings to mind Sis's stories about his supposed mental issues. But in the same moment, I'm wondering why it is that he has to be crazy just because he attempted to express his true feelings for me.

In an effort to take us back to where we were, I reach between Joe's legs and take his now-soft penis in my hand. I realize the events of the last few minutes had nothing to do with sex and everything to do with a handsome carpenter who has come to depend on me. Glancing down at Joe's head, still on my shoulder, I kiss him lightly on the cheek. "You okay?" I ask.

"I'm good," he says quietly. I'm thinking of that first night when I fell off the stepladder at his place, and he watched over me until I was able to go home.

This time, I'm thinking, was *his* time to fall.

❖

Things couldn't have been going better. I was giddy with pride and gratitude. I began to pace, and I didn't know why. I'm not talking ten or fifteen minutes of minor league pacing, I'm talking feverish pacing. Most nights I'd pace two, three hours or more from the sunroom, to the kitchen, to the living room, to the den. I felt like I was on coke. Justin and Marsala said the pacing was a discharge from all those years of eating dairy and sugar, and that it would take a while to release it from my nervous system.

"That's not the only discharge," Justin warned. "Since the carboplatin is so tough on the kidneys, the macrobiotic diet will begin to discharge the chemo from a place on the back of Tina's right leg."

And it did. Kid you not. Big, itchy red splotch on the back of her right leg.

Marsala weighed in as well. "The seemingly incurable fungus Tina's had on her toenail for the past thirty years will soon be a thing of the past."

Gone. In weeks. Feet like a Miss American contestant.

And that's not all. Justin and Marsala pooh-poohed the taking of vitamins. Your healing was meant to take place solely from the foods you eat, not from something with the potential to throw your body out of balance. And the foods Justin and Marsala were prescribing left Tina practically free of any side effects from the chemo. No fatigue or hair loss, and her white blood count remained high, something virtually unheard of with this drug. Tina looked twenty years younger, and she was swimming over a hundred laps mornings after treatments. Her cough was gone and, eventually, so were the splotches.

Our road to success would be paved with the residue of any negative energy I could put behind us. When Tina, an avid reader, had a particularly unpleasant experience with a soul-killing Book of the Month choice, I decided to take control of all literature that came into the house. Anything she put on her list, I found, read the book jackets and grilled the librarians, making sure I read at least two chapters myself, just in case there was a passage about someone dying a gruesome death from cancer.

I pushed Emerson and Thoreau over Nietzsche and Kierkegaard. I scavenged for nightly devotionals about people who scaled heights of insurmountable obstacles and read them aloud at my parents' bedside. But when it came to pure entertainment, nothing could beat the weekly headlines in the local paper. The widespread panic attributed the continuing Great Southeastern Drought was bringing out the truly bizarre in Clarke County.

THE DIXIE

July 21, 2000
<u>Crime</u> <u>Scene</u>

More Nakedness

Area officers combed Grove Hill Friday morning for a man who had escaped while in transit to the county jail. Eric Welch, who is said to be double jointed, was able to bring his hands, which were cuffed behind him, to his front, accidentally pulling his pants off in the process. He then managed to get the car window down, reach for the outside handle and open the door at the intersection of Jackson and Cobb Streets. At some point, he got into an old vehicle parked near Victory Paint & Body Shop and hid on the floor of the back seat until Grove Hill Police Officer Buster Hough found him. At press time it was still not known how the events occurred without the transporting officer's knowledge.

23

For someone who had lived with disappointment and failure longer than anyone who hadn't given up and hung themselves from a moldy shower rod, I had become a tender of miracles, struggling to keep up with all my good fortune. The old folks called it living at the foot of the cross, and for the first time I felt it: the hot red blood tickling the back of my neck like sweet salvation.

If anyone were to ask me, I'd say the most egregious practice in medicine today would have to be hands-down the unconscionable habit of sequestering the patient in those tiny cells called rooms after the nurse escorts them in.

"The doctor will see you momentarily." Of course, that can be anywhere from ten minutes to an hour and a half, a long time to sit with your thoughts and fears when you've got a cold, much less stage four lung cancer.

Per my instructions, the nurses from now on were to leave the door open until the doctor's arrival. This practice provoked a curious glance from every health care worker who passed. On this day in late August, Tina is seated in the swervy cushioned chair where the doctor usually sits, Garrett and Sis are perched on the exam table, and I am on a stool an orderly dragged in from the nurse's station.

"Well, well. The gang's all here." The physician we call Spielberg due to an uncanny resemblance and easygoing demeanor studies the X-rays on the wall behind us, something none of us had gathered the courage to do any sooner.

Garrett strokes Sis's shoulder. "We're a close-knit group, Doc. You got news, we wanna hear it."

Like a poisonous gas in the room, everyone afraid to breathe.

The doctor leans against the wall, Tina's chart across his chest. "Well, I've got some good news. The tumor is shrinking." I notice he actually scratches his head. "It's shrinking quite a bit, in a relatively short period of time."

Tina slumps. "It's…"

Spielberg takes another peek over his shoulder at the pictures. "A damned near remarkable improvement, I'd say."

Tina looks at the doctor like it's not sinking in. "So…"

Garrett leans over, taking Tina's hand. "It's good news, doll. It's—"

"Right," Tina interrupts, the truth finally registering. "Good news."

Sis takes Tina's other hand and looks into her eyes with a nod. Suddenly unable to contain her excitement, Tina stands and walks behind me, her hands around my shoulders. "This is my son, Doctor. He's a big deal out in Hollywood."

I am certain this is the happiest I've ever been in my life. "I'm not a big anything, Tina. I'm too old to be anything big."

"Hollywood." Spielberg studies me like I'm something fuzzy in a petri dish. "You're a long ways from home."

I decide I will give up cussing in honor of our news. It only seems appropriate. With whatever is happening, I want to meet it halfway with some sort of acknowledgment. It seems to fit.

"I want to stop the treatments."

"I'm sorry?"

Tina takes her hands from my shoulders, glances around at the rest of the Stalworths, then looks back to the doctor. She speaks slower this time, like she's talking to a child. "I want to stop the treatments."

Clearly, this is news to everyone, including me.

"Tina, you're doing so well. But you're not out of the woods." Spielberg taps the file in his hands with a finger. "You have stage four cancer. The tumor has shrunk, but it's not gone."

"It's my final decision." She nods quickly in my direction, as if that puts a period on the thing.

"Well," Spielberg says, "you know radiation has the potential to extend one's lifespan in many of these cases."

Tina picks up her purse, perusing the contents as if she's preparing to go. "If it doesn't come from a plant, I'm not interested. That's it, and I don't want to hear another word about it," she says, making eye contact with everyone in the room. "*This* cash cow is closed for business."

Unbeknownst to any of us, Rose O'Sharon has stuck her head in the door. "Seizure in room four, Doctor."

Spielberg continues staring at Tina for an explanation he's not going to get. She holds her purse in front of her, smiling at the doctor and cocking her head like it's a dare.

Spielberg drops his chin to his chest, takes his chart, and exits.

Rose O'Sharon squints at the X-rays on the wall across the room before looking at Tina. "Careful," she says, before leaving. Garrett looks at Tina and shakes his head before he and Sis take their leave as well.

Tina looks at the floor for a few moments before she goes out the door and into the reception area. Rose O'Sharon stands by the desk, peering down at a clipboard before glancing up at Tina, who appears to be trying to get up her gumption to say something. Instead, my mother locks eyes with Rose O'Sharon, grabs the clipboard off the reception desk, and drops it dramatically on the floor. She grabs my hand and whisks me away like we've just left a robbery note.

We call Justin and Marsala from the car to share our news with them, putting them on speaker so Garrett and Sis can hear. They remind us to remember to chew at least fifty times before swallowing, saying they can already tell by the timbre in Tina's voice that she's improving, that she is the luckiest mom in the world to have a son like me, and her complete healing is only a matter of time.

Amidst all the excitement, Garrett and Sis can't find one sour note to play on their bitter bassoons. It's all for one and one for all, and it finally feels good to be alive again.

❖

The heck with stretching—the rumor of fall teases its way across the Gulf Coast. My chest fills with the scent of dirt and pine needles as I blast out the carport door and past Jewel Ann's driveway. The doctor's warning still rolls about my head, but the sound of Tina's voice as she staked her claim in his office buzzed louder. She had given us an earful on our way home.

"All he has is his medicine. But between the diet and visualization, chanting, prayer, and so many things I can't even wrap my head around, who's gonna win this thing? And if he thinks he's gonna let his radiation burn up all the good I've done on my body, he's got another think coming!"

As if out of thin air, a temporarily energized Puffy is snapping at my heels, foam flying from her minuscule jaws.

I kick into high gear, leaning into the hill in front of me. "Can't catch me anymore, mangy mutt. RUNNIN' TOO FAST FOR YOU NOW, MEAT-EATING MONGREL—YEE-HAAAWWW!"

Puffy stops breathless by the side of Blue Cove Road. Twirling around, I wave goodbye to the hateful little terrier with both hands, running backward over the crest until she finally disappears from my field of vision.

THE DIXIE

November 8, 2000
<u>Religion</u>

Church Lock-In

Following last month's successful missions trip to Alabama Raceway Ministries in Talladega, the Fairweather Baptist Church will host on Friday night its first ever youth interfaith lock-in, with screenings of the films *Left Behind* and *The Omega Code*. The Reverend Al Tate will conclude with a sermon, *Making The Decision To Wait*. The festivities start at six p.m. and a hot dog supper will be served in Fellowship Hall.

24

There's a thing about tending miracles. You may have done nothing at all to manifest them; you just wake up one day and they're there, all bright and shiny and concrete in their permanence. And it's part of every human's natural inclination to keep watch over them night and day, because someone or something is usually waiting in the wings to make those miracles that much harder to tend. But watch we must, as the only other alternative is to simply let things take their own course.

I have taught myself in one hour what Garrett had once claimed would take a hundred. The blades of the ancient John Deere tractor break the crusty red earth into neat rows of submissive powder as I circle the trunk of the sweet gum and start all over again. Pulling weeds from the edges of my handiwork, Tina gives me a double thumbs-up, a habit she only recently picked up, a silent signal she now works into her routine as often as possible. I offer her a single thumbs-up back, since the unwieldy monstrosity I'm still mastering requires at least one strong hand on the wheel at all times.

Turning down the driveway from Blue Cove Road, Garrett steers his pickup away from the house and down to the top of the hollow, parking too close to my project for comfort. Hopping out of the truck with what appears to be a portfolio, he approaches my latest path, waving his arms like he's pulling a 747 in for a landing, hollering over the tractor's engine, "WHAT'S GOING ON?"

"PLANTING A GARDEN!" I holler with a grin.

Garrett comes over to the tractor and unfolds a set of contractor's blueprints on the ground below me. I cut the engine, glancing over the prints without a clue. "What's this?" I ask from my elevated place on the seat of the tractor.

"Plans," Garrett says excitedly, "for the camp house."

Tina walks over, attempting to look over Garrett's shoulder.

Garrett pulls her close for better viewing. "I always told you my dream would be to one day build a huntin' lodge up on Poppy's place before I die."

He was referring to a piece of densely wooded property his father had deeded him after his death thirty years earlier, a place Garrett relentlessly surveyed on foot every Sunday that rolled. Eventually he'd coerced my mother into giving up her Sundays to tread and retread the isolated area with him.

Tina answers like she's not sure she's hearing him right. "Yeaaaah."

"Well, that's what I'm going to do." Garrett puts an arm around her shoulder.

Tina is silent for a moment. "You're gonna build it *now*?"

Garrett turns a page of the blueprints, careful not to make eye contact. "Now *what*?"

Tina is stunned. She clears her throat. "I mean, with what all we've got going on."

Garrett huffs and tucks the prints under his arm. "You're doing great," he says, looking at her, then at me. "Right, Bo Skeet? Now's as good a time as any."

Tina bites her lip and looks out over the swimming pool before she turns and makes her way brusquely back toward the house.

"What's the matter with her?" Garrett says.

Unwilling to further engage with the tidal wave that is Garrett with a plan, I restart the engine on the tractor and get back to work.

❖

"Hel—heeeee-heeeeeeelp! Oh, God—HEEEEEEEEEELP!" Tossing and turning on my stomach, attempting to rouse myself from a nightmare where I'm smoking cigarettes and eating pork chops, I finally holler as best I can through the sheets twisted about my head.

"Hey, hey, Bo Skeet—"

"HEEEEL—" I open my eyes with a start and exhale another holler.

"Crap," I say, as Sis, seated next to me, comes into focus.

"You okay?" she says, sitting me up against the headboard.

"Huh? Uh."

"Jesus," she whispers, putting her hands on her face. I've never heard her take the Lord's name in vain, and the sound of it startles me. Embarrassed beyond belief, I pull the covers under my chin in silence.

Ready to move on, she motions to the bedside lamp as she quickly rises. "I'll leave this on," she says as she walks out the door. "Good night, okay?"

Still frozen, I manage a weak, pathetic, "'Night."

Two seconds later, Sis walks back in the room. "Are you seeing Joe Tischman?"

"Huh?" *How could she possibly know?*

"I saw you walking across his lawn yesterday," she volunteers, like she was reading my mind. "You had this blissed-out grin on your face, and it looked like you'd dried your hair with a cake mixer." She crosses her arms across her chest and waits for me to answer. "It's okay if you are. The Stalworths don't love like other people. You know that, right?"

Even in my half-awakened state, I am touched by Sis's

reference to Tina's words and their possible effect on me from decades ago. Maybe because she's caught me in such a vulnerable state, the ridiculousness of all the fears I've sat on all these years is staring me in the face. *Who gives a shit if I, like half the other Stalworths, don't love like other people? So what if Garrett's bloodline stops with me? What if, like Tina, I'm handed some life-ending diagnosis over breakfast one day? Would I give a damn about any of it? Would anyone?*

The sound of my bedroom door closing pulls my head out of the clouds, and I realize Sis has already made her second exit.

❖

Shaking off the remnants of my fitful night of sleep, I am huddled in the north corner of the tree house, the first shard of daylight piercing through the water oaks around me. The tang of gardenia in the air fuses with the steam from the cup of bancha tea I'm nursing. Just when I think the day couldn't get any better, I spot him for a split second, just across the creek in bright orange swim trunks and nothing else on the rebuilt Tischman sundeck. He commences what appears to be some sort of tai chi ritual. I set my cup of tea in the corner and lean into the windowsill, taking a bead on Joe with the binoculars. Although the squat roof keeps my head tucked into my chest, I make a feeble bid to reproduce his fluid movements as he welcomes the day.

"*Hey.*"

Startled out of my furtive tutorial, I grab the roof for stability and peer out through the paneless window.

"What are you doing up?" Tina looks from the ground below like a baby bird waiting to be fed.

"I couldn't sleep," I say, glancing over my shoulder at Joe, now flat on his stomach, arms outstretched before him like a long, sensuous snake.

"Me neither." Tina looks about, rubbing her arms for heat. "Are you dressed warm enough?"

"Yes. I'm dressed warm enough."

She grins. "Are you playing fair?"

I feel my neck tense and release, trying to allocate equal time and attention for these two exceptional people in my life. I laugh at Tina, suddenly in on the reference she's tossed me from half a lifetime ago. "Yes, I'm playing fair and, yes, I'll run in the house if the skeeter truck comes. Now go back to bed."

Tina smiles, waves, and heads to the house as I turn back to the now-empty Tischman sundeck and squat with my cup of tea. It's over so fast, I wonder if it even happened.

25

Tina runs her foot lightly across the pool's surface, her capris rolled up to her knees, an old photo album open across her lap. She designed and landscaped this area, and it's still her favorite spot on the property. She begins most mornings with a vigorous dip, no matter the weather. She's reminded us more than once Katharine Hepburn swam in twenty-degree temps for decades and did just fine. My father would always say the actress's tremors probably stemmed from said frigid dips.

We've been here since dusk, an hour ago now, perched on the concrete next to the diving board. Up until this point, my mother has not volunteered any impressions of the pictures she charily thumbs her way through. "Did you see your friend fixed the pool light?"

"What? Who?"

"Joe. This afternoon."

I stare at the milky glow from the bulb underneath the board, expecting to see some remnant of his surprise appearance.

"It went out years ago. I kept begging your father to replace it, but he kept putting it off, and one day I decided I liked it." She clears her throat. "Well, I *thought* I like it." Tina swishes her foot more quickly across the water and brings it down with a hard, defiant splash.

"He's quite the specimen," she says, holding my gaze with a curious expression.

"Who?"

"Well, Joe, silly. So, what's going on there?"

"What do you mean?"

"With the two of you."

Wow. This is my chance. To finally have a talk about this unexpected journey with Joe.

"Bo Skeet?" She still hasn't looked away.

And then I realize I can't. I can't tell her there's a chance she'll never have that wedding or that grandchild even if she continues to thrive.

"He's a good friend." *The Stalworths don't love like other people.* She said it. Yet this is all I have to say to her. *What am I so terrified of?* That's an easy one. I couldn't live with myself if she found the news upsetting and it got in the way of her healing.

"Oh," she says quickly. "That's nice." The moment is over. And I realize what a moment it was. My face threatens to overheat with the anger and disappointment I've pushed down.

"Whatcha got there?" I ask.

"Old photos," she says, running her finger across one of the pages. "All these folks' strengths and insecurities put together in one pose. Flicker of clarity, frozen in time. And of course, you're never aware when someone's taking your picture that fifty years later, that singular pose may forever define how someone thinks of you. Just like that. Frozen."

I glance over the edge of the album at a sepia-tinged shot of a very young Tina, her downturned mouth smeared with berries.

"I never knew how to smile when someone was taking a picture," she says. "I was always trying to figure out what to do with my mouth."

This was no news to me. Whenever we were on family trips and my father would grab the Instamatic, she'd always stop the proceedings by waving a hand. "Wait! Hang on a second. Oh, phooey!" she'd say, moving her lips this way and that. Something that came so easy for everyone else always seemed like work to Tina.

"You know, I was thinking." I haven't quite yet decided how to proceed, but I press ahead. "My whole life I've never seen you get really passionate about anything. I mean, I've seen you enjoying your painting, but I've never seen you get crazy happy about anything. There was always something tentative about your happiness. Does this make any sense to you?"

I realize as I'm saying it that I could easily be talking about myself. Tina looks directly in my eyes like she's suffered some form of betrayal. I continue carefully. "I've noticed there's this thing you do. Whenever you're angry or afraid to speak up for yourself, you clear your throat. Now, I'm not talking about the cancer, I'm talking about something you've always done. You clear your throat. Did you ever notice this?"

She doesn't say a word for a moment. Breaking eye contact, I gaze at the other end of the pool.

"Do you know that I was born at home?" She speaks calmly, quietly. "And the umbilical cord was wrapped so tightly around my neck that I almost died?" Tina stares straight ahead, playing with the collar of her T-shirt. "I still can't stand to feel anything tight around my neck."

I'm not sure what I expected, certainly nothing this precise.

"You know," she says, leaning an arm on the diving board, "when I was five, my little sister died of appendicitis. My mother and father never spoke of it again. But I needed to. I had dropped her when we were playing, a few days earlier. She was fine, but I couldn't help thinking that's what had brought on the appendicitis. I carried that thought with me every day. I think Mother knew it. That's how she kept me under her thumb all those years," she says, a tiny smile crossing her face. "I always had a hunch that I was beautiful, talented, and smart. But Mother always told everyone, 'Don't compliment her, she'll get the big head.'" Tina freezes. "When Mother was dying, I was holding her hand in the hospital room. She looked up and said, 'So beautiful.' At first I thought she was talking about me. But then I realized she was looking just *past* me. Heaven. She saw heaven!" she says, the look of genuine awe on her face swiftly chased away by a fake, upbeat smile. "How could I compete with that?"

A dead maple leaf twirls outside the skimmer. I focus on the last of its whirling trajectory and remain as still as I possibly can.

"Anyway, after I had my children, I said I would always make sure you and your sister knew you were beautiful, talented, and smart." She pushes a lock of hair out of her eyes and holds it in place. "Guess I left myself out of the equation."

After hearing this confession that answers so many of my questions, I feel I should offer some solution. It's a clumsy one. "Do you ever think about teaching? Maybe privately?"

"I think about it, sure. Let's get me out of the woods first. Okay?"

Since Tina's clearly been much more forthcoming than I have, I decide to keep the dialogue going. "I've never asked you about the hospitalizations."

"No place to put the anger," she says.

"Anger at Garrett?"

"At everything. And not just your father. Listen," she says, taking my hand. "Your father and I have been head over heels in love since the day we met. I'd take a bullet for him, as they say, and him for me."

None of this was a surprise to me. I knew he signed *All My Love* on the inside of every card he ever gave her. I always thought it so poetic in its simplicity, this declaration from a man who would tell you he hadn't read a book since high school. *All My Love.*

"Here's what I think happened. Your father came up during a certain time when women weren't given a voice. There were definitely those who *did* have a voice. Mother was one of them. It was just in her DNA. She never had to fight to find it. Your grandfather knew that's what he signed up for. Perhaps if I'd expressed my wishes early on, Garrett would have had to surrender. But I didn't. I made my bed." She squeezes my hand harder. "Don't ever make a bed you can't get out of, Bo Skeet."

I squeeze my mother's hand back, a sign I'll do my best, whatever that is.

❖

Through the smudged windshield of the Lincoln, I can see Garrett pacing inside a square of red flags near a stand of poplars marking the site of the prospective camp house. Feeling the only thing his father's acreage lacked was a body of water, Garrett hired a high-priced contractor and built a lake. Not just any lake, mind you, but a tarn as big as three football fields.

He flaunts the head of a gigantic indigo snake in my face as I slam the door of the car. "Get that thing away from me," I hiss, tumbling backward into the arms of a bay tree.

Garrett laughs and coils the thing around his neck. "Almost stepped on him when I got out of the pickup."

"Fine. Just put him back."

Garrett absentmindedly pets the snake's head and puffs up his chest, looking out over the site with pride. "So, what do you think?"

"Is this my imagination or will this be a poor man's version of the house we already have?"

"Won't be a poor man's anything, Bo Skeet."

"So, what's the point?"

Garrett leans against the electricity post and picks his teeth with a pine straw. "The point is, I'll have my own place far away from anybody else. And I'll have my *own* catfish."

"Your own catfish," I repeat without comprehension.

"Yeah. I'm tired of having to go out on that dangerous river. As a matter of fact, they're already here," he says, looking out at the lake. "I had it stocked a few weeks back."

"So you're building a house only a few minutes away from the one you already have. For catfish."

Garrett points an accusatory finger at me. "There it is."

"There *what* is?"

"That look you give me. That judging look you got from your mama."

I remember how much better I felt on the John Deere when Garrett had to look up at me from what seemed like ten miles below. Spying a rotted pine stump, I jump up on it like an auctioneer. "I'm sorry, but am I living on another planet here? The Planet of It's All about Me and Not about the Person Who Has *Inoperable Lung Cancer*?"

Garrett rolls his eyes. "I think it's time you got on back to California."

"Shit," I say, forgetting I'd promised the powers that be I'd be cuss-free forever. "I am way too fucking old for this."

"There he goes with the f-word," Garrett says, turning away from me.

Deciding I want my father even lower than he already is, I indicate a spot on the ground between us. "Please, have a seat."

Garrett turns around, threatening. "Excuse me?"

Somehow I manage not to look away even though I desperately want to. "Have a seat. Please," I say, indicating the snake. "The both of you."

Garrett looks about and sits on the ground. He lets the snake go, and I attempt to camouflage a flinch as the serpent slithers past my stump and into the thicket behind me. Garrett shows the palms of his hands. "Well?"

"Look. I know how much these woods mean to you," I say, turning around on the stump, taking in the scenery for his sake. "They're good woods. And I know how much Tina means to you, and I wanna give you something to think about. You're not gonna like it," I say, pausing for effect. "But if you build this cabin now, it will kill Tina."

Garrett offers up a half laugh, squinting at me like I'm crazy before looking down at the ground between his boots and digging one of the heels into the straw.

"And I mean literally do her in."

"Those are some strong words, son."

"But it's the truth." I realize this next part's going to be a stretch, like taking a kid from simple addition to trig in one fell swoop, but I figure I've got nothing left to lose. I take another strong bead on Garrett. "Tina hasn't found a way to speak up for herself."

Garrett blows out a chestful of hot air and jumps up.

"Sit back down!"

"What?"

I've no idea I've tilted my head back like Clint Eastwood about to have his day made. "*Now.*"

Garrett glares at me with cold black eyes. I glare back. Several interminable seconds pass before he finally sits back down.

Nothing can stop me now. "Your building this place up here is the least supportive thing you can do. All your energy will be going into it and not into helping Tina get well," I say, placing my hands on my hips. "Are you with me here or not?"

Garrett seethes, his eyes darting from me to the ground. I hear something jump in the lake below us, probably one of his catfish. He kicks the ground around him in frustration and gets up anyway. "Can I get up now, or do I have to get some kind of court order?"

Without a word, I hop off the stump and head back to the car, where I find the indigo snake coiled by the rear tire. Garrett always said if you weren't man enough to kill a snake, then you were gonna have to be man enough to meet him again. Jumping back with a gasp too dramatic to cover, I close my eyes and take a deep breath before opening them again. Eyeballing the serpent and gritting my teeth like Kirk Douglas on crank, I pick up the thing with my bare hands. It makes no move to coil around me but holds its head straight out in front, like a divining rod leading me to my target. I kneel down and let it go, watching it closely as it arches its back and disappears.

Leaving the scene, I hold the brake pedal close to the floor, revving the motor at the same time like some Hazzard County redneck. I let off the brake in one lightning-fast move, baptizing the site in a shower of dirt and gravel as the Lincoln bumps and snorts across the pig trail that takes me back to the highway.

❖

Tina, Sis, and I are seated around the breakfast table, silent, shoulders back in apprehension as Garrett bangs around the counter space behind us. Returning from an early morning marketing trip to Healthy Way an hour earlier, I'd walked into either the Stalworth kitchen or a set from an Irwin Allen disaster movie.

"Son of a bitch," he spits, slamming a kitchen drawer.

I proceed with caution, wanting to help. "You know, Garrett—"

"Don't say a word." He slams another drawer. I can smell basmati rice simmering along with something else I can't make out.

Garrett approaches wearing one of those full-body aprons with frilly piping. He places a tureen in the center of the table and turns to Tina, serious, nervous. "Madam, may I present your breakfast." He hurriedly picks up a cookbook from behind him on the bar and reads aloud. "Miso soup contains living enzymes that aid digestion and strengthen the blood." He slams the book shut and holds it behind him. "So."

Tina is floored. She peers into the tureen. "You made me miso soup?"

"I did. Would you like me to serve you?"

Tina looks to me and Sis, then back to Garrett, tongue-tied. "I'm not—yes, of course."

Garrett had attempted to make grits on one occasion soon after he and Tina were married. The effort was such a disaster, the house had to be aired out for a whole weekend. As far as we could tell, this meal was going off without a hitch. Tina, Sis, and I were positively dumbstruck.

Tina holds her bowl out in front of her like Oliver Twist.

My first instinct is to jump up and give Garrett the biggest hug he's ever gotten. But I'm not about to mess with perfection.

THE DIXIE

February 11, 2001
Crime Scene

More Burglaries, Two Gators

Sheriff Jimmy Poole reports there were two more burglaries this week involving stolen videos and magazines, one on Pine Street on Saturday and the other on Semmes Way on Sunday. Both incidents took place when the residents were away.

In an unrelated story, two alligators in a drainage ditch on Hadley were caught and killed Tuesday by alligator control specialist Gary Casper. Because of the overpopulation of alligators, and loss of their natural habitat by human invasion, it was more practical to destroy the gators than relocate them, Casper said. It is illegal to feed alligators. Anyone caught feeding them can be fined up to $500, so don't do it.

26

Ha, *what* was that?" I say, reeling from what I'm almost positive I heard Joe call me. Realizing how harsh it sounds as soon as I say it, I put a hand on his knee, trying to repair the damage. Taking a swig of drugstore wine to soften the blow, he looks up quickly, embarrassed.

Joe and I are seated cross-legged on the creek bank behind the Tischman house, a jumbo-sized bottle between us, plastic party cups in our hands. All he'd said was, "Do you want another glass of wine, love?" Probably brought on by the vino, it was over very fast.

"Sorry," I say. "I didn't mean—"

"Didn't mean *what?*" Joe says, immediately incensed. Jumping up, he walks to the edge of the thicket. "Do you have a problem with us?" he says, turning back around, making an imaginary line between the two of us with his index finger.

"What?" I'm still wondering if there's any way I can backtrack, say I meant something other than what it sounded like I meant. "No."

"Then why did you just—"

"It's not a big deal," I say, attempting to move on. "It just sounded like something my grandmother would have said to my grandfather, that's all."

He laughs, not the *isn't that funny* laugh, but the *screw you* laugh.

"You're serious. I mean, have you ever even been with another person? I mean, in any intimate way whatsoever?"

"Joe, I really think you're making a big thing out of nothing."

"Noooo, mister. *You* are the one making a big thing out of nothing." He stumbles about the bank, not because he's drunk, but because he's deflated, his buzz kicked in the teeth by my feeble insecurities.

He backs away toward the thicket, eager to get as far away from the assault as possible. "God, now I'm embarrassed, even though it was this subconscious, insignificant thing. I just thought that since, you know, there's a little something else going on here besides backslapping and basketball...shit almighty, I cannot believe I am having to justify myself here. I'm sorry I said it! I'm damned sorry I said something that was so unbelievably girly, nice and familiar."

"Don't be sorry," I say as quietly as possible.

Joe paces and shakes his head.

"Don't be sorry, okay?"

He goes deeper into the brush, the long shadows of a nearby stand of cattails masking his face from view. "Hey, you there?" I say, soft, uneasy.

Jumping to my feet, I sit on a fallen log next to Joe. "I am an idiot."

Joe turns around, tosses his empty cup into the bushes, runs his fingers through his hair, and shakes his head.

"There is probably evidence somewhere that proves I have a fair amount of issues," I say, laughing self-consciously as we finally make eye contact.

"No shit," Joe says flatly. "Bring forth some of this evidence. Something that will better help me understand whatever crazy-assed shit just went down here."

I'm thinking that's like the pot calling the kettle black, if the rumor Sis heard was true. But what I also realize is that whatever crazy Joe is or isn't or was, it doesn't hold a candle to the crazy I get when I consider showing up for someone for the rest of eternity, no matter how attractive the prospect is. I was also never any good at letting a moment be. I always had to pick at it and louse up any chance of redemption.

"I was in a bar with Frances for some benefit thing," I hear myself saying. "There were these two guys in Western gear, you know, the hats, the boots, the whole nine yards, dancing to 'Sugar Pie, Honey Bunch.' Actually singing it to each other. And I thought that was ridiculous."

"And this means what, exactly? That you're a homophobe?"

"No, that's not it at all. But the Stalworths go back and forth, see? They ruin people's lives. They can't be trusted!"

Joe is laughing. "What in the hell are you talking about?"

"Where the fuck is the wine?" I ask, fumbling over and under the log for my discarded cup.

Joe shoves a cup in my hand and pours.

"My mother told us— "

"Told who?"

"Sis and me. When we were kids. That the Stalworths don't go one way or the other. They mix it up. Get divorced, get back together, leave children. They can't ever make up their minds. You know how gay guys can't even stand the thought of eating pussy?"

"Yeah."

"Well, I love it. I could do it all day long."

"Good for you," Joe says. "So what?"

"So, I love what I do with you just as much. Maybe more than with anyone I've ever been with. And that's not allowed."

"By who?"

"The sex police, whoever."

"Well, there's the whole Kinsey scale—"

"I know," I say, "but no one pays any attention to that. I have to make up my mind or else I'll be just like one of the rest of 'em. Just another Stalworth who can't pick a side."

"Phillip. Look at me."

"And I'm too old to be having this discussion anyway, right? I'm too old for so many things."

"Phillip, stop," Joe says. "Look at me."

I take another slug of cheap wine and squint in his direction. "Why do you care?"

"Huh?"

"Why do you care what anyone else thinks? How much pussy you should or shouldn't eat or if you dream you're climbing a forty-foot dick when you sleep or if you're too old to have a career or go to the moon. Why do you *care*?"

The question hits me square between the ears, for whatever reason. I'm figuring it's because I care so deeply for the person who's asking it. I take another sip of wine and stand, walking the length of the log before I stop and turn back around to face Joe.

"I adore you." There. I'd said it. And I wasn't even aware it was coming. But I knew I wasn't just saying it. I knew it was true. So I just let it lay there like a cat who'd spit up lunch and hoped no one noticed.

"Okay," Joe says, sucking on a frond he's plucked from a cattail.

"Hey," I say, hoping for some sort of inspiration to break the mood of insanity that, strangely enough, originated from me.

"Hey," he says, like a grunt.

Willing to sell my firstborn to change course, I find myself jumping up and down on the log, the picture of anxious buoyancy, slapping my hands together, holding both out to him, an energized minor league catcher at the top of the first. "Hey, look. Here I come."

Joe looks at me like I've gone completely around the bend, which, of course, I have.

"Catch me." And with that minimal ounce of forewarning, I jump on the guy and he seizes me, having no other choice but to hold me like a big, fussy infant. "See?" I say, looking down on my bewildered, handsome Jewish boy with a giggle. "Now this is far more ridiculous than anything I've seen in a leather bar." The ice officially broken, I wrap my legs tightly around Joe's waist, checking his demeanor with a raised eyebrow.

Stifling a laugh, he gamely plays along, hoisting me an inch higher for his comfort. "You won't *do*, boy" he says. "Dude—slick—cap'n," he mocks, carrying me up the path toward the dark house on the hill. "Crazy-assed motherfucker."

❖

Justin and Marsala said a discharge would begin when Tina would begin releasing the cancer from her lungs, and it did. She expelled buckets of thick, copious mucus from her throat every morning like clockwork. Tina would sit on the edge of the bed, her focus on a tiny framed picture of a beaming Christ on the dresser, a smile of victory on her face as she spat ream after ream of paste-like gloop into a trash can between her knees.

We were told a macrobiotic diet causes drastic weight loss in most people, and more so in people with cancer. This is supposedly a good thing since cancer cells live in fat. When I have to pull up the waistline of my jeans while putting away the breakfast dishes, I realize I've lost almost as much weight as everyone else in the family.

Garrett and Sis have lost twenty-odd pounds apiece, and Tina has lost thirty-five, something she had previously concealed from her medical staff by placing weights in her sweatpants before appointments. Checking my reflection in the stainless steel wok, the only surviving relic I'd somehow neglected to send to the electrical appliance boneyard, my blurry gaunt face stares back at me.

While Fanny and I are scrubbing pans from a broccoli tempura lunch, I glance through the window at an energized Tina pacing purposefully on the front porch, her face stuck in the pages of a tiny paperback.

"What's up with her, Fanny?"

"I think that's some of *your* voodoo."

Per my directive, Tina is reading a book written by a Santa Monica psychologist about the triumphs of a handful of her patients who, upon receiving the news of their cancer, took control of their lives and figured out the exact point when they gave up their personal power and chose cancer as a way of getting out of their misery.

Tina slams the book shut, thrusts an arm of victory in the air, and makes a beeline from the porch into the kitchen. Leaning against the pantry door, she holds up the treatise. "Thank you for this. You were right, it's incredible. I mean, a shrink who might actually know something, who'd'a thunk it?"

Tina had an extremely low opinion of shrinks. The one who'd overseen her treatment years ago, Dr. Robert Watkins, had slept through most of her sessions. In later years he became the go-to witness on many high-profile sanity hearings, which she found wildly unsettling.

Tina tosses the book on the counter. "The fact that some emotional event, or even a lifetime of spiritual neglect—that's what she calls it—can—I mean, shit—I can't even talk about it yet." She blows through the back door like a human tornado. "I'm going for a walk. A long, long walk."

Hanging up the dish towel, I call after her in disbelief. "Did you say *shit*?"

❖

Sis was in town for her high school reunion. Little did she know the real blowout would be at home. Within minutes of her arrival, she, Garrett, and I are seated against the flood wall of the patio like a jailhouse lineup, Tina pacing back and forth in front of us like an aggravated warden. "I've been doing some thinking, and if I'm going to get well, then I have to remember who I am. I always painted—when I was a kid, when I was in high school, and I was good at it. People loved me," she says, stopping in front of my father. "But then I met you, Garrett Stalworth, and I bore your spawn."

Sis and I freeze in unison. This is going to get worse.

Tina paces some more, her eyes still glued on Garrett. "And when I wanted to study in Mexico that summer with the children, you said, 'What will it look like, your going off to God knows where to do God knows what? What will people think?' Oh, and I listened, and I heeded. And when I went to work at the Center when the kids were in high school, *you* refused to do the dishes because you said *you* made more money than me."

Tina had worked for a year at a day home for mentally challenged adults, and she had loved it. At some point she became a mentor to the mother of one of the clients, attempting to empower the woman to leave an abusive marriage. Shortly thereafter, Tina had another nervous breakdown and resigned.

"And I started to cave, ashamed at my selfishness in wanting you to help out around the house," she says. She stops again in front of Garrett, really starting to lose it. "Feeling like I didn't even deserve to be an integral part of the working world." She leans in inches from his slack-jawed face for effect. "But I was making a difference in the world, which is more than I can say for a pharmaceutical executive, in my opinion," she hisses, turning to face me. "How am I doing, Bo Skeet? How am I doing, Sis?" she shrieks, her voice a decibel higher than I even thought possible. "No cough, last time I checked. NO COUGH, GARRETT, *SEEEEEEEEEEEEE?*"

Tina throws a scarf around her neck like Eleanora Duse finishing a great scene and heads into the house, slamming the door behind her. Garrett crosses one leg over the other one and says "Hmm" to no one in particular.

That night, she chanted her name at the top of her lungs from behind her locked bedroom door till the wee hours: *Tina, Tina, Tina, Tina.* Sis and I read in the sunroom until it was over, and Garrett fell asleep in his La-Z-Boy. He was still there the next morning.

❖

Joe had invited me up to his place to barbecue to celebrate our two years of dating. He never called it an anniversary—probably because he thought I'd go ten different kinds of insane.

The felled cedar beneath the creek infuses the night air with the fleeting whiff of Christmas. Having wrapped up dinner an hour earlier than I'd planned, I decide to head out. Walking across the backyard of the Tischman place, I stop to watch a quartet of foxes playing underneath the security light behind the garage. Each of the foxes holds his own place in a formation resembling a small baseball diamond. As one of the foxes runs to the fox on the next base, the tagged fox sprints to the next, and on it goes. To this day, it's the most astonishing thing I've ever seen in the animal world. And I've never told a soul about it. I must have been watching the game for five minutes when I hear something from inside the house. At first, it sounds like Joe's laughter. *Must be on the phone.* But in the next outburst, I detect a clear note of distress in his voice and I realize he's crying.

Thinking I should move furtively to avoid breaking up the foxes' game, I begin curving up to the house. But when I hear another outburst, I make a beeline to the nearby sundeck. As I head up the steps, I can see the tails of the foxes scatter to the bushes on the other side of their makeshift diamond.

"Anybody home?" I ask, opening the door an inch or two. The inside of the house is dark, except for the stove light in the kitchen. Torn between wanting Joe to know I heard him and pretending I didn't, I call out again. "Joe? You here?"

A few seconds pass before Joe materializes in the hallway entrance. "You're early," he says.

"I know, sorry," I say, startled at his disheveled appearance.

"It's all right," he says, camouflaging his emotional state with a yawn. He rubs his eyes like a kid after a nap. "Come on in.

Let's put some lights on and get this barbecue thing on the road, shall we?"

"You bet," I say, still standing in the back door, afraid to disturb the air in the sorrowful place.

❖

"I'm sorry," Joe says, placing his half-eaten veggie burger on the wooden patio table. "I'm afraid I'm not good company tonight." He props his feet on one of the wooden benches built into the sides of the deck.

I hold up the bottle of wine over his glass.

"No, thanks," he says. "I don't think I should."

"Can I ask you something?"

"Well, you can ask," Joe says, "but I can't guarantee I'll have an answer."

For a second, I consider making something up, scrapping my intention to probe the situation. But before I can back out, I'm already forging ahead.

"I heard you earlier tonight. You sounded very upset. And I'm sorry I heard you. I had no business coming here early. Maybe I should have gone home. But I'm here. And I want to know if there's anything I can do."

Joe sucks his teeth once, twice, like he's figuring a math problem.

"Do you want me to go?" I ask. Listening to his soft, rhythmic breathing, I watch his chest rise and fall. He still hasn't looked at me. "Hey," I say, placing a hand on his forearm, golden brown from all the days working outdoors. "What's going on? Joe. *Tell me.*"

He doesn't answer.

The minutes tick by, but I still can't manage to make myself leave.

"Several of us, we were acclimating before we took

Manaslu," he says, "with some high-priced guide from London." He reaches for the wine bottle and pours.

He doesn't say anything else for a good while longer.

Then he downs the cup in one gulp.

"That glacier, man, that was the most beautiful thing I ever saw. Like some big, dodgy bowl of sugar and diamonds. The whole thing could have gone at any minute."

I can tell from the recurring silence that this next part is going to be hard for him.

"And Kyle, he got skittish. You could see it in his eyes. He wanted to go through with it, but he couldn't. Said he had a feeling. So he stayed behind..."

Joe's voice becomes harder to understand. It's like he's talking to me from another planet.

"And we went ahead...with the rest. And he...he never made it back to camp. It was almost worse than actually seeing him go, you know?"

Joe is now speaking over his shoulder in my direction. I breathe a tiny sigh of relief, grateful he's finally including me.

"He just wasn't there. Like smoke, there was something in the air. It seems uncommon, I guess, to hear of someone dying that way, but if you climb, you know a lot of people who..."

Joe holds up five fingers. "Five people died on the mountain that year. He was one of 'em."

For a long time, neither of us says anything. There are no tears from Joe—all cried out, I guess. My tears are another story. Getting up from my chair, I walk directly behind him and dry mine on the sleeve of my shirt. Not once during the story was I ever thinking this was what sent him over the edge. In fact, I was so shaken by the harrowing tale, the thought wouldn't cross my mind for another day.

I put my hands on either side of his head, tilt it back, and kiss him on the lips.

"Would you do something for me?" Joe says.

"Anything."

"Hand me the other half of my burger?"

I grab the plate and sit in his lap. He groans like I'm too heavy, but I ignore him.

"Here," I say, pulling off a bite of the burger. "I'm going to feed you this burger like you're a fucking ancient Egyptian king."

"Ha. I will *not* let you feed me like I'm an ancient Egyptian king." He takes a slug of wine. "Okay, maybe I will."

"Sire," I say, holding a piece of burger in front of his mouth. As he takes it and chews with a weak, closed-mouth grin, I know better than to think the joviality of the last couple of minutes has scared away the spirit of a long-lost love. But at least we both know he's there.

THE DIXIE

May 10, 2001
Crime Scene

Man Shot Dead in Casket Store

Ferris Drinkard, 68, of Chancey, suffered multiple gunshot wounds to the head and was pronounced dead Friday morning at Casket Emporium in Trinity Village Shopping Center.

Harry Gates, 70, of Dukes, who was treated for minor stab wounds, was charged with the murder. He was taken to Pugh County Metro where he was being held pending a bond hearing.

"Drinkard and Gates were business associates at one time," said Chancey police spokesman Dewey Rotch. "They've had disputes over business matters in the past," Rotch added without elaborating.

Rotch was unable to say whether the two men were still business associates or whether their past association was in the casket business.

"It's a terrible thing," Rotch said. "The business of death is tough enough without heaping added strife and discord to the mix."

27

Two years and three months had passed, and I had still not left my parents' home in Alabama. For the first time in my life, I felt as if I had actually taken control of a situation and accomplished something worthwhile. I wanted nothing in my way to thwart that success.

My mother was, for all intents and purposes, a different person. When Tina smiled, she now seemed to expect the world to smile back. And if they didn't, then screw them. I felt I was the catalyst for that change, and walking away from her at this delicate time didn't seem right.

Weeks flew by as quickly as the hand on my travel alarm clock ticked off seconds, always set just past dawn. This way I could log in my daily diary on my laptop, an undertaking that had become the most important part of my day.

The drought continued across the southeast. Lakes and rivers were drying up. Two-hundred-year-old oaks were dying at the root. There were times we had to run for cover in the heat of the day to avoid the swarms of thirsty bats coming to drink from the swimming pool. Naturally, it fell on my shoulders to net out the furry dive bombers that didn't make it. Allergies were at a peak the medical community had never seen. But we no longer had allergies. Colds and flu, Justin and Marsala said, would be a thing of the past.

I had never seen an unshakable faith like Tina's. She never cried, never worried, never questioned. I fed my faith by staying in constant motion. I was always bringing something new to the table. I felt like the buck stopped with me, and it was my task to keep all of the balls in the air.

Tina wanted to go see her doctor to request he turn over her files so she could burn them in effigy on our next visit to the Village. A few days before the appointment, we heard through the grapevine Rose O'Sharon's only child had been killed in a terrible car accident on her way home from college. I wondered whether the incident would affect the nurse's worldview, not to mention her bedside manner.

When the day came, I was entering the medical center from parking the car after having dropped Tina off at the door. As I rounded the corridor, I saw a strange sight. Tina was holding a withered Rose O'Sharon, who looked like she'd lost everything she held dear. I watched for a moment, feeling very uneasy. Rose O'Sharon pulled away from my mother, reeling. She must have been on some sort of tranquilizer to help her cope. After an unbelievably kind and understanding Spielberg sent us on our way with his blessing, Rose O'Sharon stuck her head out the door. "Y'all take care, now," she said empathetically, with a slight smile, before hollering down the hall in the other direction. *"Hey, Wanda, we need a death certificate on Mr. Lo, stat!"*

Ah well, guess some things never change. But to say things were through changing around the Stalworth house would be an understatement. Only two years in the business, Sis was suddenly selling more houses than she could count but still spending every other weekend with us so I would get a break from my duties. Her Brittany spaniel, once an aging layabout, was now eating an informal version of the macrobiotic diet. Vacating her doghouse at dawn, the revitalized mutt disappeared to chase squirrels and didn't return until dark.

The phone started to ring. People wanted my help. I was asked to pay a visit to the ex-wife of a local politician. Laura

Holden was bedridden, desperate, and in a great deal of pain when I arrived. Her family was at her side: her son, daughter-in-law, sister. Her husband had divorced her months earlier, and soon after she was diagnosed with advanced stage pancreatic cancer. She motioned me to sit at the foot of her bed.

Clearly once very beautiful, the disease had left her weak, brittle, and bitter. "He asked to come back after I got sick. I told him I didn't want anything he had. That included him." She winced, looking longingly into my eyes like she thought I held the power to raise the dead. "I'll do *anything* to get rid of the pain."

This wasn't anything I had planned—to minister the sick? Still, I offered what I could. The family looked on as I shared stories of those worse off than Laura Holden who had bounced back, prepared a simple meal in the adjacent kitchen, and unloaded stacks of books, one of which translated the word *Macrobiotic* into *Big Life* on its cover. Her mother sneered like I was a high priest in some Tinseltown cult.

I left the house on cloud nine. I was officially spreading the gospel. Not only was I guiding Tina's life, I was now guiding the lives of complete strangers!

Shortly thereafter, a morbidly obese cousin began dropping in to watch me prepare my food. An old friend from high school who had prodded me into sharing my macrobiotic knowledge called at six a.m., nattering on over the ear-splitting racket of a vacuum cleaner. "I just have one question. Does your head ever feel like it's gonna blow off 'cause you're gettin' so clear? 'Cause mine does. My whole damned *body's* vibratin'. I feel like I have the gift of prophecy. And it's telling me if I eat one more fermented soybean, I'm gonna leave that sorry-assed husband o' mine. You know what? I think I'll do that anyway, *as of right now*."

Big life indeed.

28

I am tiptoeing through the living room with two fistfuls of crinkly Walmart bags past a snoring Garrett.

"Hey, Bo Skeet," he grunts, eyes shut tight.

"Shh!" I say forcefully, the only surefire way to get an extra ten minutes of silence from the sleeping lug.

He snorts fiercely and conks out again.

"Shit damn hell."

Sounds like Tina's voice from down the hall. I drop my bags on the floor of the living room.

"Shit damn hell. Kiss my ass."

This one's Tina, no mistake. I take a couple of careful steps down the hall.

"Eat my tuuuurds...Hmmm, okay, hold on," she says, like she's trying to get something right.

Entering the master bedroom, I am met with what appears to be a giant pile of clothes, pillows, and shoes Tina has tossed from her walk-in closet. When she appears around the door, her forehead is wrinkled in concentration. "Turds. Why don't I know that word, Bo Skeet? And shitass. I think that's my favorite," she giggles, going after another load. "Shitass."

I follow her inside the closet and watch her snatch a pile of sweaters off the top shelf.

"I am reinventing myself," she says, swiping an armload of

cocktail dresses off their hangers. "I'm getting rid of everything that doesn't work for me anymore."

"Good for you!"

"Cathy and Dana are going to teach me how to cuss."

Cathy and Dana are Tina's walking buddies, neither of whom have a lick of trouble speaking up for themselves.

"It's been a year and a half since I stopped the chemo. I'm a new person. My life has to reflect that."

I have nothing to say. Everything that comes out of her mouth is music to my ears.

Tina blows the hair out of her eyes and heads back out to the bedroom. "I'm not even sure I can stay married to your father. Hell, I may go to Mexico and never come back." Tina heads back into the walk-in and stops. "And another thing. I want to worship with a group of people who are more about life than about death." She walks over to the bedside table, takes up a notepad, and waves it in front of my face. "I've made a list of alternative worship venues," she says, pointing to one on the list. "This guy? Rumor has it he was run off by a neighboring Baptist Church for having New Agey thoughts. I thought you might want to come with me to check him out. What do you think, huh?" An impish grin slides across the face. "Sounds like one of those California things."

❖

"It's more of a slow, steady rhythm," Joe says from behind, his hand over mine, guiding the reeling mechanism on the fishing rod. My feet dangle over the swamp below the pier, his legs on either side of mine.

"You're kidding me, right?" I say incredulously.

"No, why?" Joe's voice teases the back of my neck like a waggish dragonfly.

"Do you know that I was called Kingfish as a child because of my fishing prowess?"

"You were not," he says, trolling the line, pulling my hand gently up with a tug.

"You ask anybody."

"I will. I'll ask anybody as soon as we're done here. And I'll bet you a jillion dollars you were *not* known as Kingfish due to your fishing prowess."

"We'll see," I say with a chuckle.

"So…um…I'm done here. With the house, I mean."

I am aware of the slackening in my grip as the words hit me. "What?"

"I'm done," he says. "With my folks' house."

"No, you're not. It's still a mess."

"The finishing carpenter'll take care of that," he says. "Look, Bo Skeet. Ordinarily, I'm a fast worker. But I stretched out a ten-month job here to two frigging years. And I sure didn't do it because I love Clarke County." He pretends to look for something in the tackle box.

We'd never had a conversation about how long his job was taking. And I'd never thought about it. "So. What are you—"

"I've got another job. Over in Jessup. A big place. And I need to get started on it. I have to work."

"In Jessup." I have to remind myself it's only an hour from here.

"Yup," Joe says, pushing the hair out of my eyes. "And I'm leaving in a few days."

"A few days?" The thought of our time in this jacked-up Eden we'd created coming to an end is almost more than I can stand. "I don't even know what to say to that."

"And after that, I dunno where I'll be," he says. "I was thinking maybe eventually even California."

He's back in the tackle box.

I try and focus on my line, pretending I've heard nothing. The suggestion that he'd even consider joining me in California makes me feel light-headed. I suppose I've had too few wonderful surprises in my life.

"What do you think about that, Kingfish?"

"Hmm?"

The control freak in me is already trying to figure all this out. In the time since I heard his anguished cries about Kyle, I wondered if I could ever compete with that. I've pictured Kyle the essence of perfection, inside and out. And then there's me with my fears, neuroses, and love handles. No comparison in any way, shape, or form.

My intuition tells me my time here with Tina isn't finished. And besides, Joe didn't *definitely* say California. I am overwhelmed.

"You got a bite, there," Joe says, pointing to my line. "On your reel. A fish."

"Shit!" I say, sitting up straight.

"Easy." His hands lightly shake out my forearms like a fistful of wet lettuce leaves. "Not so fast. Give it some play."

Ignoring Joe's advice, I yank fiercely on the line, a battle of wills more between myself and the man behind me than with the pathetic creature fighting for his life. Joe removes his hands from the top of mine and several seconds pass before I belatedly detect a loosening in the line. I watch the fish blissfully skate the surface of the swamp before disappearing into deeper waters.

Joe squeezes the tops of my shoulders. "Better luck next time, Kingfish."

"Dang." I toss the rod down next to me and crawl out of his lap.

Joe grabs me hard, climbing on top of me.

"Cheeky know-it-all," I say, kissing him on the mouth.

"You didn't answer me," he says, pulling back. "About California."

Damn. Now he's acting like it's definite or something.

"No," I say with a reassuring smile. "But I will. Okay?"

"Okay," he says, with a look of disappointment and a half-hearted peck on my lips.

"Look," I say, placing my hands around his neck. "I like the sound of it. I do. But I still have so much going on here. I mean, I don't even know when I'm going back."

"Okay."

"Can I tell you something? Something really crazy? I'm scared if I leave now—"

"Something will happen to your mother."

"I bring the food, the books, visualizations, the chants—"

"Her entire life is in your hands, and your hands alone."

"Yup, crazy. Just like I said."

"Any mother would be lucky."

"To have a nutcase son like me," I say.

"Well, it comes from a very good place," Joe says.

Joe repositions himself over me, and one of the slats of the pier underneath us shifts. I glance upside down at the russet water of the swamp swirling like a giant mud bath below. My heart tumbles to my feet like one of those high-rise theme park rides where the floor drops out.

"Careful," I say, about so many things I don't even know where to begin.

THE DIXIE

August 25, 2001
Home & Garden

Love Hurts

It's that time of year again, and lovebugs—those ubiquitous conjoined flies that seem to gravitate toward windshields—are out in force. The *Plecia nearctica*, found from Costa Rica to the Carolinas, emerge from the larval stage in the fall to mate, thus the current infestation.

"They do not bite, they do not sting and they do not carry any diseases that we know of," said Kelly Micher, an entomologist with the Mobile County Health Department. In the morning, unsuspecting males will swarm once conditions are warm enough. Females wait below for the swarm and then fly through it. The males grasp their lady loves in flight and the pair falls to the ground and couples. At first they face the same direction, but after coupling is completed, the male turns 180 degrees. Then they fly with the female, who is larger and in control.

29

Hey, wanna see a backflip?" Tina calls from her new purchase, a mini-trampoline, as I clean fish on the back porch.

"No. I do not. We've done well staying out of hospitals these days, let's keep it that way."

"Spoilsport!"

Garrett jumps out of his pickup, covered in mud from head to toe. Tina does a pseudo-jackknife to show off. "Where you been?" she asks.

Garrett holds up a portfolio for the world to see. "Had to meet Glen Dayton out at the site. They pour the cement tomorrow. I tell you guys, a more splendiferous camp house you will never see."

Since Garrett had never mentioned the camp house after our come-to-Jesus in the woods, I assumed the project had been called off or at least postponed.

He rubs his belly and dances a little jig. "Hoo, boy. I feel like a kid again." Garrett walks up the steps, pokes a finger in the ice chest full of catfish, and pulls back with a fake holler like he's been finned. Laughing, he winks at me, turns around to wink at Tina, and goes inside.

I run my hand absentmindedly down the outside of the ice chest, unsure of where to look, what to say, or who to say it to.

Tina jumps for another couple of seconds before she hops off the trampoline and heads up the back porch steps with lethal determination.

I steady myself for a moment before reaching back inside the chest—*snap!*

I pull my hand out just in time, a big blue missing my finger by only a hair.

❖

Garrett covertly opens a drawer below the top shelf of the bookcase. Slipping out a piece of candy, he unwraps it, pops it in his mouth, drops into his La-Z-Boy, flicks on the TV with the remote, and reclines, smacking like a cow chewing its cud.

The back door slams as Tina enters, talking to no one in particular.

"Be damned if I will," she says, grabbing the remote from his hands and turning off the TV before tossing it on the sofa out of his reach.

Garrett swallows the candy with a gulp. Without so much as a sideways glance in his direction, Tina storms the bookcase, pulls the bag of chewy candies from the drawer, and shakes them violently in his face. "I *know* you've been hiding chocolates, and I just wanted to say thanks for the support."

Peeking in from the back door, I try to make myself small.

"Keep up these bad habits and you'll be heading down for a dose of carboplatin. How would you like *that*, mister?"

Tina empties the entire contents of the bag on Garrett's head and blasts past me on her way down the steps.

Garrett peers up at me through the mound of cellophane before he sheepishly pulls a piece of candy from inside the collar of his work shirt. "Hey, Bo Skeet," he says, like a ghost.

❖

Since Tina was doing so well, Sis had invited me down to her place in Pensacola for the weekend. After I led Tina through a tour of the bins of grains and bags of greens labeled for her convenience in the Stalworth kitchen, she had finally ordered me out the door. "I'll be fine," she said. "You need a break. Go have fun!"

"We got this, Bo Skeet," Garrett says, gnawing on a piece of seaweed.

Sis had a new girlfriend. We went to her house the first night for dinner. They danced and made out in the kitchen while they cooked dinner. Feeling like a third wheel, I played with the surly Maltese in the living room until he bit me.

"When are you going back to L.A.?" Sis says later that night over surprisingly good pasta and shrimp. "Tina is fine."

"It's time you got back to your own life," New Girlfriend says, with a hand on Sis's back.

"I don't know. Soon."

"Is it Joe?"

"Joe had to take a job. He's gone."

"Oh," Sis says. "Then I'm sorry. Or whatever."

"So," New Girlfriend says, "now you're *truly* free to go back."

"I guess so," I say, glancing in my napkin to see if the wound from the dog bite has stopped bleeding.

"How exciting!" Sis says.

"Is it still bleeding?"

"Oh, um," I say, not really hearing her and noticing the dog shooting me a nasty look from the love seat. I shoot him one back.

New Girlfriend has put her fork down, gazing at me with eyes of genuine concern. "Is it?"

"No," I say. "It stopped. I'm good."

❖

I've rigged an old work shirt of Garrett's to shade the glare of the sun from my open laptop. The whiz of the fishing rod in its holster heralds movement on the other end of the line. Grabbing the rod, I set the computer on the pier next to me.

Needing some time to myself, I'd driven up to Garrett's lake. Since he had a dentist appointment that afternoon, I knew I'd have the place to myself. I was relieved to find I could decompress underneath the shade of the cedars.

"Whoa, bro," I say, more to myself than to the fish, letting the indomitable bastard take the line into deeper currents. On my way to the lake, I'd caught a glimpse of Joe taking the duffel he'd never unpacked to the pickup in front of his parents' place. As far as I was concerned, stopping to say goodbye wasn't even an option. I'd pushed every thought of his leaving to the back of my mind. I couldn't begin to fathom the depth of suffering this separation could bring. I remembered staring at the ratty duffel in the corner of the room from the warmth of Joe's arms, wondering if it had been with him when he lost Kyle.

I hadn't paid him a visit since he'd given me the news, and I was conscious of the damage my absence could be creating. One day I had decided to make my way to his place but tripped on a pine branch in the middle of the path and became completely unhinged. I jumped and kicked at the brittle limb for what must have been two minutes. Catching my breath and whatever was left of my wits, I realized I'd come to depend on him in ways I was too terrified to count.

Sis was right, I decided. Since Tina was doing so well, it was time for her to fly on her own. I would pack my bags and return to the Golden State. And contrary to what my former agent might have to say about it, I did, in fact, have a life back there.

"I miss you more than you deserve, you little shit." Caroline's voice crackled through the cell phone the night before. Her speech was peppered with the language she always directed to L.A. traffic, a habit that wore on my nerves.

"Please don't cuss traffic while you're talking to me. You know how that grates."

"Sorry."

"So, I think I'm gonna be coming back. I mean not right now, but soon. And I don't want that to mean anything." I wondered what she could be thinking on her end. I knew it sounded harsh and insensitive. I couldn't imagine she actually missed the black cloud that hung over our relationship those last couple of years. I know I didn't. Still, it had been a union we both had found difficult to sever.

"Oh. Well, sure," she'd said. I could tell she was making a valiant attempt to remain neutral.

"I've been seeing someone," I said. "He's...well, he's a Joe." Although there was a pause, this couldn't have come as a big shock to her, as we'd had more than one conversation about my family history and my place in it.

"Oh, uh-huh," she said, unconvincingly nonchalant. "And how is that?"

"I think I screwed it up. The whole thing terrifies me. You know how I am with these things." I threw this out because I really needed to talk about it with my best friend.

"Look, I've gotta get out of the car," she said. "I've got a class."

"Oh, sure."

"So, whenever you decide you're coming back, just call and let me know and I'll pick you up," she said before she hung up.

The tugging on the fishing line brings my attention back to the task at hand. I focus on the cunning creature fighting tooth and nail for the chance to awaken another day in the muddy sludge of the swamp's bottom.

I recall that, as I passed the Tischman place, Joe glanced briefly in my direction with no sign of acknowledgment. Too many days had passed with no word from me. The cliché about the pit of one's stomach being the resting place for longing and denial proves truer than ever. I actually felt a pull in my solar plexus, like I was finishing off a set of crunches.

"Easy, buddy," I say, letting the diving, swirling fish take its prize even farther away from the pier, my eyes falling on the handle of the rod in my lap, the line unspooling like unbridled thoughts released to some cold, black infinity.

❖

Tiny plastic crates of purple petunias and bright pink zinnias line the front seat of Garrett's pickup. Tina wanted something to brighten the sunroom in the late summer stubbornly lingering on the Gulf Coast. Having taken Blue Cove Road northbound from town for some time now to avoid the sight of the Tischman place, today I find myself entering from the opposite direction. Slowing the truck to a virtual crawl as I approach the house, I spot a thin, lively-looking couple who must be Joe's parents taking luggage from a late-model BMW. The sobering sight reminds me of the one miracle I'd practically kicked to the curb.

I continue on before I could decipher which one Joe got his graceful good looks from.

Sometimes when we're weak, we can only handle one miracle at a time.

30

I am awakened this morning the same way I've been awakened in this house for as long as I can remember: by the sound of my mother creaking the loose floorboard outside my door on her way to the kitchen. How she manages to step on the same weak place every single time, when the rest of us are unable to find the spot even when we try, has been one of our many family mysteries.

A few minutes later, I walk into the sunroom to find Tina talking on the phone. With a hand over the receiver, she whispers that a macrobiotic pal of ours from the Village had just called to inform us Aveline Kushi, the mother of macrobiotics, had died. Of cancer.

By early afternoon, I was yelling into the landline, hidden in the bushes behind the pool. "What do you mean calling and telling Tina that? Do you know what irreparable damage you've done? Are you some kind of idiot? Your phone calls are no longer welcome here…whoa, yeah, I'm serious."

To my relief, Tina proves to be less affected by the news than I am. As I walk into the basement that afternoon, she hollers through the whir of the exercise bicycle she is riding. "I think she was just calling because she wanted me to be aware that some people, even though they eat the food, don't do the emotional work needed to heal. That was obviously the case with Aveline. I mean, everybody knows her past," she says, like some bitchy New Age guru.

❖

Marsala says Tina's fruit has to be cooked before she eats it, which makes me feel guilty for the one-in-your-mouth-five-in-the-bucket ratio for raspberry picking. Still, the sweetly sour morsels are so tempting, I keep forgetting to knock the Appalachian dust from them before popping them in my mouth.

As a general rule, I stand a good distance away from Tina and Marsala during harvesting of any kind, as their conversations lean toward the deeply personal. But I never stray too far away in case Marsala offers up another of her bromides, usually by throwing a warning sideways glance in my direction.

Tina sets down her bucket at the next bush and wipes the sweat from her forehead with the back of her hand.

Marsala hands Tina a crumpled kerchief from her pocket. "But you see, Tina, finding your voice isn't all about yelling and stamping your feet. It's about living your life the way *you* want. You may not like the fact that your husband is building the cabin, but we're all wired differently. Maybe that's the way he takes care of himself, so then he can take care of you." She laughs. "And make the miso soup."

Tina clears her throat, fanning her flushed face with her shirttail. "It's hard, isn't it? Using your voice, I mean. Your *full* voice. All the time."

Marsala walks away to empty her pail into the nearby vat. "Can be."

Joanne, a woman in her late fifties and a longtime Village visitor, ambles into our row and begins picking next to Tina. "It's a hot one today. This drought'll kill us all, or at least the berry crop." She inspects a shriveled berry left too long on the vine in the scorching sun. "Never thought I'd see more than a year with not even a drop of rain."

Tina coughs like something went down the wrong way.

Joanne turns, placing a hand on Tina's shoulder. "Are you all right? Can I get you some water?"

"I'm fine. So, you had lung cancer?"

"The worst kind. Stage four. Like you."

Tina gives the woman her full attention, trying to shade her eyes from the sun, her hands red from the berries. "How long?"

"Twelve years."

"That's wonderful!" Tina beams. "Do you ever get to the point…"

"Where every time you cough you don't think the worst?"

Tina nods. Joanne takes her hand. "You can't play into the fear. It's just like this raspberry bush. How much time do you think it spends fretting over whether that dark spot on its trunk is terminal root rot or not?"

Tina laughs, coughs again, faltering a bit like she might faint.

Joanne catches her, calling to me and the others. "Can I get some help here?"

Marsala appears with a bottle of water. "Probably just some misplaced energy." She calls to Justin, who races down the hill from the house. "Let's schedule her for a shiatsu!"

❖

Justin and Marsala decided the toxic fumes from the mosquito trucks could be the cause of Tina's cough. I had gone to grammar school with the head of public works in the county. Having spent part of one summer at this fellow's family beach house as a kid, I knew him well enough to invite him over for lunch.

"Awright, I'm gon' tell you all what I'm gonna do. From

now on, when that skeeter truck turns down Blue Cove, I'm gonna have him turn off the fumigator, but I'm gonna have him leave on the motor so's the neighbors won't think they're bein' skimped on the pesticide. Awright?"

They don't call it Southern hospitality for nothing.

31

Tiptoeing down the dark hallway to my parents' bedroom for the bedtime devotional, the scene stops me dead in my tracks. In their big four-poster bed, Garrett is rubbing Tina's back, holding her carefully in his arms, gently turning her over like some tiny, priceless figurine. Tina points to a place above her shoulders, and Garrett kisses the spot before he inhales deeply behind her ears and lays his head on the pillow next to her, glancing up at her like a kid. I'm wondering if they know how damned lucky there are. To have shared your bed with someone for over forty years.

A few minutes later, climbing into the inner sanctum of the tree house, retrieving the binoculars from their place on the wall, I survey the Tischman place through the woods. I kneel on the window sill, my prayerful pose wasted on the cold, hard reality that my adventure here with Joe has come and gone.

The water ripples in the creek below, and a light in the Tischmans' carport comes on briefly. A figure crosses from the house to the sundeck and back again. I distinctly hear the back door of the house close a couple of seconds later. I can even hear them bolt the latch, a cold, deafening sound that echoes across the darkness.

I stay here, on the sill, half in and half out of the tree house, half in and half out of slumber, in the shadows of the giant live oak limbs until the quarter moon above me goes to bed with everyone else.

❖

In the six months since we'd been spared the bug truck, Tina's cough persisted. Although never heavy, its mere presence weighed heavy on all of us. On a phone call to the Village, Justin and Marsala said, "Healing isn't a straight path. The cough will come and go, maybe for years to come." Tina was happy with their response, and none of us brought it up again.

In the weeks to come, Tina developed a pain in her shoulders and lower back that never let up. At night before bed, I'd give her an hour-long neck massage, silently sending every healing mantra I could come up with. I'd read that near the end, cancer often spreads to the bones. But we'd all heard stories at the Village of people who had given up all hope before their health turned around. Sadly, everything we'd heard from the medical community offered nothing but a minimal extension of life, minus any quality to go along with it.

Sis asked Tina more than once if she wanted to see the doctor. "You could do both, right? Macrobiotics along with Western medicine. Best of both worlds." Tina's answer was always no. She refused to take anything for the pain, continuing to stay true to the macrobiotic lifestyle.

I wanted desperately to believe the diet was still working. But I also wanted to save my mother's life. I asked myself, if it was me, would I stick strictly to macrobiotics, forsaking all medicine in the process? My answer was, at that point, maybe I'd also do radiation. Sis later told me she was haunted by the fact that she didn't push the radiation more. But no matter how concerned we were, Tina had to make her own decision. My mother chose a path very few take, a path I put in front of her, and we were golden for a couple of years. Not one of us would trade anything in the world for that magical time.

When the pain increased, Sis and I drove her up to the Village. Sis asked Justin and Marsala if it would be helpful to them if Tina had a CT scan. "This way," Sis told Tina, "you won't *really* be seeing a doctor. You'll just be forwarding the information to your macrobiotic counselors, here." I wasn't against the idea. But Tina would have none of it.

Justin and Marsala said, "We don't need a CT scan to do our work. Tina is on the healing path. She is fine. Nothing has changed."

So, that was that.

❖

Garrett and Tina are glued to the TV when I come in from my run. Hovered over a steaming bowl of miso soup on a tray, Tina coughs hard into her dinner napkin. She doesn't look well. I take a seat on the hearth in front of the blazing flames of the roaring fireplace, the consequence of an unseasonably cool fall.

"Your aunt Lola called, said we needed to watch," Garrett says without looking up from the cable news show. A faith healer in her eighties is being interviewed by the respectful host.

"So, the irony was, as a healer, you were finally faced with this horrible, incurable illness."

The faith healer smiles, leaning across her side of the desk. "A study proved people who were prayed for by others fared better than those simply praying for themselves."

"And you believe you were healed because of the thousands of people praying for you all over the world?"

"Beyond a shadow of a doubt." The faith healer turns to the camera, closes her eyes, and raises a hand. "Jerry, I just want those in need to come to the TV and lay their hands on the screen. God's unconditional perfection, I can feel it, is now moving across the airwaves. Just do as I say right now. Crazy as it sounds. Take my word—all of you."

Tina pushes aside her tray, pulls herself up out of the chair, and makes her way slowly to the TV. She kneels in front of the screen, her hands crackling with electricity as she lays them on either side of the faith healer's head.

"Lord, I just want you to come into these living rooms right now, and I want them to feel the goooolden light of your heeeealing salvation lift them up. Can you feel it?"

As if on cue, a spark of fire discharges from a splinter of kindling and out on the carpet runner next to the hearth.

Tina looks at me, then to Garrett, an eyebrow raised in wonder.

"*Can you feel it out there, people? Can you feel it?*"

32

The GPS proclaims the news from the dashboard: *2694 La Grange, you have reached your destination.* Easing the Lincoln down the red dirt road past a dry creek bed, I cut the engine next to the massive framework of a home nestled in the edge of a bluff populated with towering white oaks and longleaf pine.

Joe appears from around the rear corner of the house with an armful of yellow lumber.

"Siri gives shitty directions," I say, stopping to keep from running head-on into him.

Stunned, Joe stares me down without expression. "Yes, she does."

Feeling as though I should, in some ridiculous way, offer to help with the lumber, I opt instead to simply nod, fruitlessly attempting a smile. "How's it going?"

Joe turns, continuing past me around the corner of the house. "It's okay."

"Listen," I say, following. "Wait up."

Joe calls over his shoulder, catching me glancing up at one of the construction workers hammering on the roof directly above us. "Don't worry," Joe says, "Javier doesn't speak any English."

Javier's English-speaking smile doesn't go unnoticed. "Maybe there's a place we could talk."

"Sure, Phillip," Joe says, throwing down the lumber and taking several long strides away from the house. "How far away would you like to get? Huh?" Joe turns and walks even farther away from the site, stopping next to a box of roofing shingles. "How's this?" He takes a few steps more. "How do you feel about Memphis? Is *that* far enough?"

Hearing him call me by my given name for the first time, I am even more mortified and self-conscious. Moved by the degree to which he clearly cares, I'm acutely aware of my lack of ability to repair the situation. After kicking the dirt beneath my feet for a moment, I step over the scattered two-by-fours to get closer.

"What happened to you?" Joe says. "After that day on the pier, I never heard from you again."

"I'm sorry," I say, thinking I could have found a more original response.

"Sorry and what?" Joe says.

"Tina's not well," I hear myself say for the first time to anyone.

Joe takes the news in for a second. "I'm sorry to hear that," he says, and I can tell he truly is.

Doing anything possible to break his pitying gaze, I take a seat on a nearby sawhorse. "And I don't need you to do anything or say anything. I just needed to tell you."

The silence from behind me is deafening. But I asked for it. I pat the empty place next to me on the horse. "Take a load off, would you?" I say quietly.

Another moment of stillness before he comes around and sits. His hair, now shoulder length, makes him look less like an aging basketball star and more like a college student playing the lead in a freshman production of *Godspell*.

"You know," I say, "Mama Louella used to tell us if we had too much on us, we'd get a pass on anything. You could pretty much commit hari kari but if you said, 'You know, Mama Louella, I've had a lot on me lately,' she'd say, 'Whoa, sugar, that's all right,' and all would be forgiven."

"You can't turn people and situations on and off like that, Bo Skeet. You understand that, don't you?"

For a moment I feel as if a piece of my gut has been removed with a dull blade. "I do now."

Hoping it's not enough to scare him off, I carefully reach up to finger the curly locks hiding half his face. "I like this hair."

"I just forgot about it, I guess."

"It looks like you did," I say, pulling my hand away before he asks me to. "Listen. It stunned me when you said you might come to California. And when I say stunned, I mean I was awestricken. The thought that you would even consider that made me happier than I've been in years. You always see in movies where people will go, 'I can't see you anymore. I'm scared.' And I always called bullshit on that. I mean, what the fuck? Someone loves you, someone really terrific, and you leave 'em because you're scared? But I get it now. I get it because I want it so badly. And all that's going on with Tina? It was just too much." Feeling as if I may cry, I dig my thumbnail into the palm of my hand, hoping to relocate the emotion to a more neutral place. "I thought maybe you'd go to Jessup and forget about me."

Joe shifts his feet, and I can tell our precious time is almost up. "Well," he says without looking at me, "that's a lot of information you've just given me. Thank you for being honest. You know, Phillip, honesty is a good trait in people. Without it, others can never feel they can trust you."

"I know that," I say, willing to do almost anything to prolong our time together.

"I've got to get back to work," Joe says. "And you need to go get back to Clarke County and forget about me."

Scooching over to hook my arm in his, I lean in to press my face against his shoulder. It smells like turpentine and sawdust.

"What are you doing?" He says it with an air of annoyance because he's supposed to, not because he's annoyed.

"Just sniffin'," I say, pulling him close.

Joe pats my hand, jumps off the horse, and begins gathering the scattered pieces of lumber.

"You know," I say, standing, "you're the first person outside my family to call me Bo Skeet—I mean, since I was a kid." He glances at me out of the corner of his eye. "The first time you said it on the porch that day? Boy, the show was over for me."

Figuring I'm roughly six seconds into overstaying my welcome, I do everything in my power to push down the importunate *Please tell me not to go tell me to sniff all I want kiss the back of my neck like you do when I'm asleep*, but I know it's coming out for sure if I stay, so I head back up the red dirt road. When I turn around to look one more time, I catch him looking back, too.

When I get back to the Lincoln, I find myself thinking of a movie I saw when I was a kid. It was called *Let's Scare Jessica to Death*, and at the ticket office Mrs. Bailey, the manager of the theatre, gave out cards with an inkblot of Jessica's face on the front. The gimmick was if you stared at the image long enough, you could then close your eyes and the tormented heroine would appear on the inside of your eyelids until you opened them again.

Before I start the engine, I shut my eyes tight to see if I can still see Joe Tischman's big soulful eyes looking back at me, but I can't.

THE DIXIE

September 1, 2001
Articles from Our Files
115 Years Ago Today

September 1, 1886:

Our county jail now contains 11 prisoners—a pretty large family for Sheriff Chapman.

One of the heaviest rains that ever visited this area, considering its duration, fell on last Monday about one o'clock. The Cobb grist mill, a mile east of town, was carried away, dam, house, and all.

Tony Pace, colored, residing near Whatley, dropped dead Saturday while walking the road. He only remarked to someone with whom he was walking, "I must stop," and, sinking to the ground, immediately expired. There was no inquest.

33

I was now running over twelve miles a day. I ran more than I slept. Running was the one thing I still felt I could control. I could say I was going to run fifteen miles when I left the house and do just that.

Once I even ran all night. When I stopped just outside the carport the next morning to tie my shoe, Puffy ambushes me from out of nowhere, snagging a hunk of flesh from my index finger before dashing away to hide, shivering, behind the monkey pine.

Which is just about the time when I hear a rustling from inside the Little House. I peek in, and there, next to the riding lawn mower, is the smallest alligator I've ever seen on dry land. It's not tiny by any means, capable of doing *some* sort of damage, but probably not to me. Mind you, this sort of thing happens all the time on the Gulf Coast. Every member of my family has posed for a snapshot with at least one errant gator, which is crazy considering we're some distance from the river, but the timing here is damned near awesome.

"Heeeeeere, Puffy, Puffy," I call out, crouching low to reach her on her own terms.

Puffy eases out from behind the tree, weaving, growling.

A genuine smile starts at the core of my being, a joy at being alive in times of heaven-sent spontaneity.

"You want some of this good stuff, Puffy?" I hold out my hand, pretending I'm eating something beef-tinged and yummy.

She puts her right paw forward but takes it back before it touches the dirt.

I hold out the imaginary contents of my hand in Puffy's direction. "Yeah, you want some of this stuff," I say, pretending just how tasty it is.

She responds more enthusiastically this time. One of her ears even twitches.

"Goooood stuff, Puffy."

Still crouched, I open the Little House door behind me and toss the make-believe food inside.

Like the entry of the gladiators, the ugly little motherfucker sprints over the threshold. Slamming the door behind her with a whoop, I plaster my back against the frame, laughing like Vincent Price in one of those Roger Corman films from the sixties.

Crashes and bangs reverberate from inside the Little House as Garrett, netting dead leaves from the pool, calls over the fence. "Is everything okay over there?"

I offer up a weak, transparent, "Yes, good!" I can hear imaginary crowds cheering for me and all I'm doing for mankind in this singular moment in time. One giant leap for bad dog-haters everywhere. I clasp my hands above my head—World Champion.

I can see Garrett go back to skimming.

"Here, Puffy, Puffy, Puffy." I can just make out Jewel Ann's crackly voice as I look over and catch a glimpse of the old lady standing on her front porch with a broom. "Heeeeeeere, giiiiirl!"

More crashes and bangs from inside as I jam myself even harder against the door.

Jewel Ann looks directly at me, goes back to her sweeping, then looks at me again with genuine concern in her face. "HEEEEEERE GIRL!"

Eat my turds, lady.

A furry paw makes a quick, pleading motion under the crack of the door between my feet.

Shit. Not such an unpleasant paw without the ugly-ass face attached to it, I suppose.

Damn hell. I glance back across the road. Jewel Ann is no longer sweeping or calling. She's just looking at me. Like I'm evil incarnate. Which I'm not. But her shit-eating ugly-ass dog is. Crap, I don't even think alligators like dog. I just wanted to see what it would feel like to drop something into hell's mouth and watch it try and squirm its way out. Or not. That's the thing about hell's mouth, you never know.

I bask in my victory one last second before I grudgingly open the door a few inches. Puffy bolts out of the carport like gunshot from a .22.

Opening the screen door for her beloved pet, Jewel Ann waves appreciatively just before she attacks a spiderweb over the porch light with her broom. Smiling, I wave back like the world-class champ I am.

❖

The flat, white package I take out of the mailbox bears a striking resemblance to one of the First Baptist Church yearbooks I've collected with the rest of the bills since I've been home. But upon closer inspection, I see the parcel is addressed to me. Easing myself down on the battered silver culvert by Blue Cove Road, I tear into the box. A brightly colored hardback titled *Know Your Lures* stares up at me from paper bag wrapping. On the jacket, the silhouette of an old-world fisherman reels one in. I pull open the front cover; no inscription from the sender.

I hold the book close to my nose and sniff hard. To my disappointment, it doesn't smell like Joe at all, only a slight new book scent. A car passes, waves, I've no idea who. I close the book and hold it flat out in front of my eyes, squinting from the side so the title bleeds into nothingness, like a clean, colorless landing strip.

Looking at the book on the pillow next to me in bed that night, I go back and forth on what the gift portends. Since Joe didn't sign it, this might be his way of bringing some good-natured closure to the whole thing. *It was swell. Take care.*

But as I'm drifting off, I'm thinking of the first night I spent at Joe's. What a fool I made of myself. Lying on the ground, drenched in beer. And he's directly over my face. *Can you breathe?* he asks—

And I wake up with a jolt. Like a visitation from someone still among the living, the pseudo-dream leaves me feeling like a wartime amputee who still feels pain in the limb they've lost.

I'll have another chance with Joe. I've no idea when it will come. Maybe six months, maybe five years, but I know without a doubt I will. It may not even be a good chance. It may be the shittiest chance anyone ever got. But I'll have it.

Turning off the bedside lamp, I'm out again before my head hits the pillow, and he is situating a pillow behind my head and a blanket over my beer-soaked body.

"Okay, brother?" he says.

I nod and pull the blanket over me like a squirmy toddler.

34

Two years after Tina raised that severely ailing rooster from the dead, he took sick again, but this time through no fault of my own. I again took him to my mother, expecting another miracle. But this time she made no move to do anything other than close his eyes with a gentle touch. "Safe journey," she said. And that, unfortunately, was that.

On the occasion of my birthday, I am weeding the garden when Tina and Sis drive up. They had sneaked off early in the morning without a word to me. A clearly shaken Sis approaches, followed by an equally distraught Tina. "Tina wanted to get an X-ray, so we did. The cancer in her lungs has spread drastically. The doctor says the macrobiotics are no longer working."

Tina looks at me and shrugs her shoulders like she always did when the answer lay somewhere in the cosmos.

Within minutes, Sis, Garrett, and Tina are preparing an enormous breakfast of eggs, bacon, and burned cinnamon toast in defiance.

The four of us are gathered around the table, ogling the greasy food.

"Just goes to show you, Tinker Toy medicine from California," Garrett says, shaking out his checkered napkin.

The daggers in my eyes stop Garrett cold.

Tina glares at me across the table. "I think I want some

cheese. And some jam—no, make it syrup," she says, speaking to Sis but still glaring at me. "No grace today, Bo Skeet."

Sis passes the syrup directly in front of my face.

I decide not to look at anything but my plate. "You had to sneak out for the X-ray?" I say. Tina looks down at her plate. "You don't think I would have approved?" I shove away from the table so fast it sounds like the glass cracks in the French door behind me. "I will *not* be made to feel like this is my fault. Because it's not. You're all acting like twelve-year-olds. And this is *not* my fault!"

I throw my napkin down on the table and try not to step on the wrapped birthday gift next to my chair as the real twelve-year-old leaves through the good French door.

❖

The next day the terrorists bombed the World Trade Center. The day after that, Tina started a new brand of chemo. But first she had to endure a procedure to remove the fluid rapidly collecting around her lungs. During a thoracentesis, a needle long as a butcher knife would be inserted into Tina's back and into her chest cavity, drawing out the mucus her lungs were now floating in.

On our way into the hospital, the front page of *The Dixie* screams, "Threat Of New Terror Is Serious."

Rose O'Sharon meets us at the door. "Y'all come on back and have a seat," she says over a stuck-pig grin. "We been expecting you."

Entering the inner sanctum, it's damned near impossible for the four of us not to take in the walls of the hallways already decorated for Halloween. Nothing like a cancer ward full of cardboard ghosts, goblins, and skeletons to remind you of your impending mortality.

A handsome technician who looks just like an African

American Jesus kneels next to Tina in the waiting area of the radiology department. "Now, Mrs. Stalworth—"

"Call me Tina."

"Tina. What we're going to do is we're going to stick a needle in your back to remove the fluid collecting around your lungs."

Garrett looks away. Sis puts her head in her hands. Having banished the chief executive assistant in me to exile in light of recent events, I focus on a nearby potted plant in order to avoid eye contact with any of the more levelheaded decision-makers in the familial hierarchy.

"We can't put you to sleep because you need to stay awake while we do this. That way you can take some deep breaths for me while I perform the procedure. Okay?"

Tina stands and follows the technician. I also stand, but my feet are frozen solid to the freshly buffed linoleum beneath them.

The technician turns and smiles. "Would you like to come with her? You can wait just outside her room."

I wait while Tina sizes me up. With a nervous smile, she almost nods. I follow them in.

❖

While I'm waiting, I notice that, unlike my travel alarm clock at home, the second hands of every single one of these titanic-sized hallway clocks appear to travel in the worst kind of slow motion.

"Now, Ms. Stalworth, how are we doing so far?" the technician asks Tina from inside the room.

"Good. I'm good." She sounds more brave than scared, almost defiant, which raises my spirits higher than I would have thought possible.

Another technician, a woman, says, "*Now* how are we doing?"

A noise from Tina—a tiny cough, then a big one—"Oh, Jesus, oh, no. Oh, Jesus, you're killing me!" she shrieks.

In seconds, my morale plummets. My mother is in serious trouble, and there's nothing I can do to help. I want to climb the wall and tear the second hand off the clock with my bare hands.

"Please don't—oh, my sweet Jesus *you're killing me*—"

During this moment, the world I had created from the ground up with its food, its books, and its macrobiotic gurus forever capsized.

One of the technicians, not handsome Jesus, had punctured Tina's lung with the needle, and it had collapsed. We learned this happens in about 30 percent of all cases.

As they roll Tina into the next room on the gurney, her face flushed from a lack of oxygen, the four of us surround her. Garrett holds a compress to her head, Sis massages her feet, and I hold her hand. After making a waving motion with her free hand, we are finally able to make out a faint whisper from Tina. "You are all *suffocating* me."

The three of us look at each other in horror until we realize Tina is attempting, as best she can, to break the glacial frost in the room with humor. Garrett releases a big bass "Ha!" like somebody slapped him hard on the back. Tina even manages a smile at her quip. Sis and I finally join in, the laughter coming easier after this close brush with death.

Attempting to clear my head in the hallway, it occurs to me that while we're so busy trying to control our destinies, maybe that's the most we can hope for. That if someday *we* have to endure some god-awful, suffocating, physical torture, we're surrounded by some sort of family, be they blood or not, to suffocate us with something else.

On our way home, Tina asks to stop by McDonald's for fries and a shake. I place the order myself through the car window.

❖

Two days later, Garrett begins construction on the camp house. From my bedroom window, I see Tina turn briefly from a blank easel as he blows her a kiss on his way out to his pickup with the blueprints.

Sis informs me Tina is no longer speaking to Justin and Marsala, or as Tina now refers to them, the shitasses. I, on the other hand, have dialed their number in the hopes they've forgotten some minute but invaluable detail.

"So, you guys didn't notice anything the last time we came up? I mean, come on, y'all, that's a lot of cancer not to have seen," I say, practically daring them to come up with something.

"You know, I've always thought it would take Tina seven years to heal," Marsala chirps. "I did the math, and what with her inability to assert herself in situations of—"

"Okay, you know what?" I'm not even sure what I'm going to say, so I finally settle on, "Blah." There is silence from the other end. It almost feels good to quiet the constant cacophony of recipes for endless teas, baths, and compresses pledging miracles no one has proved since the dawn of man. "Okay?" I say, like there's anything they can agree to. "*Blaaah!*" I hold the phone out in front of my face, barking like a dashboard bobbledog. "BLAH-BLAH-BLAH-BLAH-BLAH-BLAH-BLAH."

I slam the phone down in the cradle, shaking with rage and disappointment.

❖

In early October, my mother begins to lose her mind. When I return from my run one evening, a desperate Tina meets me at the door.

"There is bomb in the oven and a volcano erupting in the swimming pool." She turns to Garrett and Sis, who are standing in the kitchen door. "The only place to hide is in the car."

Radiation treatments would start the next day to kill the cancer cells in Tina's brain, although I wondered if you were going to go, wouldn't you want to be as unaware of the whole thing as possible?

"There is a Russian spy in the Little House," Tina says. "I don't know what he could possibly want with me."

"You don't worry about him," I say, putting my arms around her protectively. "He's as good as dead. Okay?"

Tina rests her head on my shoulder. "Okay," she says, unconvincingly.

35

After shopping in co-ops and health food stores for two years running, I noticed all "normal" grocery stores smelled like laundry soap, even the produce section. To this day, I still get queasy walking through the sliding glass doors of a supermarket.

Smuckers, Lay's, French's, Del Monte—the bright, colorful, squeaky-clean shelves call out names I haven't heard in ages as I make a sorry-assed attempt to steer the wobbly-wheeled shopping cart behind Sis in the Jackson Super Delchamps.

Heading down the oral hygiene aisle, Sis looks to her left, then to her right, then stops, unable to move. Her posture founders as she stumbles back a step, abruptly pitching forward in the same beat as she catches herself on the shelf with the palms of her hands like a Mardi Gras drunk.

"Why am I looking for dental floss?" she grunts, squinting at me with a pained expression I've never seen. She makes a grand, sweeping gesture across the mouthwash and the Pearl Drops. "Thousands were killed in the Trade Center, we could all die of some horrible, senseless disease even if we don't smoke," she says, crying in quick, staccato spurts, combing the shelves like a mother looking for a lost child, "and here I am looking for dental floss. It's no wonder we age, start to fall apart. It's all just too much to take."

I can see the butcher behind the meat counter halt his

consultation with a sharply dressed businesswoman. Sis flails her hands about her sides like a demonic washing machine, her shrill voice croaking in the upper registers. "Shit, man," she says, rubbing her forehead like she's been attacked by some unseen swarm. "Happiness from clean teeth?" she asks no one in particular.

She takes a deep, weepy breath and tosses her head back. Thankfully appearing to pull herself together, she shambles down the aisle before her sandal catches on nothing, and she gives the floor a swift kick. "Fuck you, America," she says in a voice too loud for her surroundings. "*Fuck you*, store." She kicks the floor again.

I dare not move. I suppose to everyone else, this terribly theatrical playlet would portend nothing but angst and defeat. But if my own recent experience has taught me anything, it's that the human animal can only stand so much of one emotion before it automatically goes the other way. It's the way we're wired. There's even only so much joy we can take before we sabotage a good thing.

So, I take two steps over to the hand soaps and wait for the flip side.

At the end of the aisle, a mother holds back her little girl like Sis might be rabid. Sis looks at the woman and then to me with a half-aborted snort, something she's always done when something terribly funny sneaks up on her from out of nowhere. I laugh out loud, something I've always done when she does it.

That night I fell asleep to the sounds of my mother and father softly singing from the confines of their pitch-black bedroom.

"Aaaand heeee walks with me
And he talks with me
And he tells me I am his own
And the joy we share as we tarry there
None other has ever knoooown—"

—from an old Baptist hymnal my great-grandmother had bequeathed us. It was the saddest, sweetest sound I had ever heard.

❖

The next morning I find Garrett slumped at the patio table, crying softly over the unopened newspaper in front of him. "She said she's ready to go. I said the days'll fly like that," he says, snapping his fingers hard, "before it's time I come on myself."

Taking a seat next to him, I stare at my hands folded in my lap. Since I hit thirty-five, the days have slipped far too quickly to suit me, and when I've hit sixty, as Garrett has, the years would surely pass like one of those time-lapse calendars from a silent movie.

"The lake is losing water."

I'm not quite sure I've heard him right. "What?"

"The lake up at the camp house. I had it tested beforehand to make sure the soil had enough clay to support the water. But something went haywire. I don't even know if I'll be able to save the catfish." He takes the newspaper, swats it hard at the side of the patio table, and turns away. "God knows I do love that woman."

I decide not to say I told you so. He doesn't need me or anyone else to remind him sometimes even the best-laid plans won't hold water.

36

One night Tina and I sat on the ground in the garden, waiting for the promised rainstorm that would bring an end to the drought we'd endured for so long now. Our hopes were firmly in check since we'd been promised the storm many times over the last two years. Watching the last of the season's fireflies float about the bluff, their dull green glow a polar opposite of the bright yellow mating dance of the early spring, I remembered collecting their magic in Mason jars as a kid. I wondered if it would be worth it. If someone said to me I would have to endure round after round of chemo and thoracenteses to see another season of fireflies on a balmy night, would I do it?

"A few months after I married your father, some doves nested outside our kitchen window. Only one of the babies had hatched. And one morning I went outside and a snake had gotten into that nest and killed that baby bird. The mother and father were still milling about in shock. Oh, I was furious!" she says, fingering the neck of her sweatshirt. "I sat next to that nest for hours with your daddy's shotgun waiting for that snake to come back. But the funniest thing happened. Before that day was over, would you believe that pair of doves started moving what was left of that nest out to another tree across the way?" Tina pulls a shawl up over her shoulders. "I always wanted to believe in reincarnation, you know? Come back as a bird? Now, I don't know."

A clap of thunder peels across the Tombigbee in the distance.

Tina is suddenly galvanized. "You know, I used to be so scared of thunder, but then Mother taught me this game. See, if you count slowly from the first boom of thunder until you see the lightning flash, that's how far away the lightning is. If you can count to three, the lightning is three miles away."

Surveying the equation for the first time in eons, her childhood memory makes total sense until I do the math in my head. "That's not it," I say carefully.

Tina cocks her head, unsure where I'm going.

"The lightning comes first. You count from the lightning, you wait for the thunder."

A moment of silence passes before Tina takes this in with a quick gasp. "So, you mean I've been doing it wrong my whole life?"

I keep quiet, as the way she scans the night sky tells me this revelation may be about a great deal more than storm warnings for her.

"Well," she says after a few interminable moments. "I guess it's too late for me to get all those years back."

Another rumble tumbles from the heavens, this one closer. I think of Saturday mornings in L.A. and how I would awaken to the reverb of the dumpster as the garbage man wheeled it back into the subterranean garage underneath my apartment. During my first years in California, I would inevitably mistake the sound for rolling thunder, only to throw open my curtains to find yet another godforsaken, flawlessly sunny day.

A bright flash illuminates the hollow below the garden like a snapshot as a final clap of thunder tears across the creek, shaking the earth beneath us.

And then—my hand to God—it starts to rain. Anyone from the South knows that moment at the onset of a good rainstorm when all you hear is one really loud drop, then one more, then another, like some divine deity is leisurely pelting the earth with tiny lead weights.

"Well," Tina says, her eyes shut tight. "I don't even think I *believe* this."

It rains buckets, it rains torrents, the tall pines bent in the wake of heaven's grace. Neither of us makes any attempt to move from our places in the cold, wet dirt.

❖

Two years after her diagnosis, Tina, Sis, and I climbed the highest point east of the Mississippi. The macrobiotic higher-ups had never seen anything like it. We planted a flag, picnicked on the ground, and asked a stranger to take a picture. In the picture I still have taped to my refrigerator door, we are tan, thin as hell, and healthy as horses. This, I believe, tells the story. However it all ended, we had this time. A time when most in her place would have been too sick from treatments to climb out of bed, much less climb a mountain. Tina thrived. As did we.

Tina adamantly refused any pain medication of any kind, including aspirin, until the last few weeks. I'd always thought of her as so fragile, but looking back, I know I could never have been that brave. Perhaps she wasn't the wounded bird I'd always thought.

And did Tina die, I wondered, because she couldn't speak up for herself, or did some microscopic by-product of mosquito-killing DDT lodge itself in her lung years ago, waiting to carry out its destiny?

I can remember a time when I'd have given anything to have the answer to that question. But the longer I'm on this earth, the fewer answers I seek. At a certain point you stop asking.

❖

On Thanksgiving Eve, I was helping Tina brush her teeth, something she'd lately forgotten how to do.

"Okay, so now you just need to spit," I say behind her shoulder.

Tina laughs and shakes her head.

"What do you mean?" I ask. "You don't remember?"

Tina looks out the window at nothing.

"No, look, Tina, that's okay." I gently turn her head in my direction, turning over in my mind how one actually demonstrates the task of spitting. Sidling up to the edge of the sink, I lean over and pretend to spit the biggest wad of toothpaste ever to hit porcelain. Wiping the imaginary spittle off my chin, I say, "Yeah?"

Tina nods obediently and pees on the floor. "Uh-oh," she says, like a child.

I kiss her hard on the cheek, take her hand, and wait for the flip side.

❖

That night, coming into the home stretch from a run, I see the ambulance leaving the house, passing me on its way out of the neighborhood, bouncing like a top on Blue Cove Road before it disappears around the wooded bend. I stop, petrified, hands on my knees, listening to the high-pitched wail of the fading siren.

At the hospital, Sis tells me that Tina had choked on some water and gone into a semiconscious state. "The doctors want to know how we feel about resuscitating her if it comes to that. I asked him what he would do if she was his mother, and he said he wouldn't fight it." She picks at the fabric on her chair. "I just keep thinking if I hadn't given her the water."

"Don't think about that for a second," I say, placing a hand on her shoulder, already certain that glass of water was the steady hand of providence.

❖

I wasn't quite sure how we found we'd been transferred to a hospital suite that resembled the digs of a decent hotel. I was unaware there were any rooms like this in *any* hospital. I wondered if all people were delivered to these oases just before they met their maker. I later found out Garrett had made the call. I had told him and Sis I would stay the night with Tina, and that they should go home and get some rest.

"Mr. Stalworth, I think you'll want to come in here now."

The nurse's stage whisper rouses me from one of several catnaps I've taken during the night. I have been privy to the rattle of her unconscious breathing since yesterday afternoon. A Sting song I've never heard before plays on the speakers in the hallway and I realize that, up to this point, I haven't heard music of any kind on any of the other floors we have stayed on. Clearly, this is some kind of rebel cancer floor.

Although I feel I'm being told point-blank by the nurse to hurry, the first thing I think about in my groggy state is Tina's admonition that we prevent our bare feet from touching the germ-ridden hospital floor. I scour the area below me in the darkness before I finally dig my toes into a pair of flip-flops, and breathe a sigh of relief.

The room is lit by only two lamps on either side of the bed, which lends an air of comfort. With a weak smile in my direction, the nurse adjusts one of the monitors over Tina's bed and holds out a vacuuming tube. "Do you want I should do more suction, or just…"

The rattle in Tina's throat is much more pronounced. I'm trying to think on my feet. "Of course. Well, if you think it will…"

The nurse points to a monitor. "Her heart is failing."

I don't know what to say. "Oh my goodness." Without thinking, I hop on the bed next to Tina, taking one of her hands, brushing the damp hair out of her eyes. I speak close, softly, praying silently for a few extra seconds before my mother dashes off so quickly. "Hey, hey, hey…"

Although Tina doesn't appear to be responding to the sound

of my voice, I ignore the beeping monitors overhead and talk as if we're swapping early morning pleasantries over the breakfast table. "I had dropped off just now. You know that weird place where you're not really sure it *is* a dream? You and Garrett were, like, thirty years old. We were driving in the desert. You guys in the front and me and Sis in the back, in that old Falcon we had with the hole in the floorboard? And Garrett turned to you, and he said, 'Hey, doll, remember that time you were sick and Bo Skeet came home?'"

A weak smile crosses Tina's face, the kind you see on an infant that makes you question its authenticity.

"Okay, then," I whisper.

Tina closes her eyes and exhales for what seems like an eternity. I call to the nurse without looking away. "Is she okay?"

The nurse briefly touches my shoulder, turns off the monitors with the flick of a switch, and leaves.

I am still holding Tina's hand in mine, and I'm no longer whispering. Maybe it's because we've been left alone, just the two of us, to chat as we wish. I'm suddenly recalling a passage I'd come across while thumbing through some highbrow arts magazine in one of our many waiting rooms. "Did you know that it is a literary cliché not to remember what your mother's hands look like?"

I study her hand closer, holding it up to the glow of the nearby lamp. The one word above all I want my mother to hear as she leaves this earth is the one her own mother chose to never call her. "Beautiful," I say, leaning in to make sure she hears me, as if the events of the last few seconds had been delayed due to technical difficulties. "You. Mama."

I had heard about the unpleasant scent people carried shortly before they passed, a sort of biological tell that portends imminent death. But when I hold her hand to my face, she smells just like she always did when she kissed us good night, like lemons and lotion and pool chlorine all swirled into one.

A few minutes later, I open the big picture window on the

opposite side of the room. Kneeling on the floor, my elbows on the ledge, I inhale the early morning sea breeze, looking out over the hospital lawn as the sun prepares to heave itself up over the Gulf of Mexico for one more day.

As I begin to pack up our things, I notice one of Tina's eyes has slowly opened. Roaming the suite to collect a pair of bedroom slippers, a hand mirror, and a tube of lip balm, I watch her watching me from whatever corner of the room I'm working. Like the eyes of a prostrate Mona Lisa, they seem to follow me everywhere I go.

Thinking from some loopy place that she may have come back after all, I shake myself out of it, walk back over to her bed, and take her other hand. This time it's cold, white, and stiff. I remember Caroline saying even if I didn't heal my mother's body, it would all still be okay. And even though it *wasn't* okay, it's interesting how the universe sneakily prepares you for gigantic emotional blows that would have before seemed unfathomable in their scope of destruction.

Knowing this would be the last time I would ever see Tina's body, I think of all the things I *wanted* to say. How hard we tried, *she* tried, how random life is, how I'd never look at another beautiful thing on this earth and not think of her. But, oddly enough, the only words that come out of my mouth are: "Dress warm, play fair, and for God's sake, run in the house if the skeeter truck comes."

I close her eyes. "Safe journey," I say, and I leave.

37

Someone said to me, "You jumped off the edge of the earth. You went back home and you lived for two and a half years. What did you learn?"

Well. I suppose I'm at war with my spiritual self. I still can't manage to pray. It's not because I don't think God is there, it's just my earthly needs and his way of delivering his take on them rarely match up, so why bother? The Buddhists believe we would live more peacefully if we gave up hope, and I can see their point. But there's just something about that feeling of hope, the adrenaline rush of wanting so badly for a situation to turn out a certain way. Even that feeling you get when those hopes are dashed. Just comes with the territory.

Looking back, I suppose I lived everyone's worst nightmare, watching something horrible happen to someone so close to me. And I guess what I would have to say is this: When faced with some dreaded path—and chances are, at some point you will be—jump valiantly, feet first, into that hot fiery hell, eyes wide open.

For me, within the awfulness lie things that will, for the rest of my days, defy description: brief snippets of light, love and terror, of ugly dogs and chemo nurses, macrobiotic gurus, bayou healers, and handsome carpenters. And hard as I try to put it all together, to create a sum out of all the parts, the most I know I will ever get is a nudge, a hunch, a phantom voice from some far-off place counting backward for all of us.

❖

We had a memorial for Tina at the First Baptist Church in Jackson. Regardless of her ambivalent feelings about the place, Tina had many friends in the congregation, all of whom had been kind to us in those last days. After Garrett nixed the notion of anyone singing any sad old hymns, my cousin Raquel played and sang everything from Bach to Joni Mitchell and Aretha on the big pipe organ. In the receiving line outside the church, Caroline, wearing a long wool coat far too warm for the Gulf Coast in any season, pressed my hand into hers as she gave me a kiss on the cheek.

"Frances called me. I'm so sorry," she says.

Caught between my present reality and the old one, I wonder for the briefest moment what part she played in my life. I recognize her, but almost three years have passed since I've seen her bright, fresh face and touched her warm, delicate hands, her fingers longer than mine.

"My God," I say, realizing that my time gone has added a couple of crow's feet around the edges of her big brown eyes. "When did you get here?"

"This morning," she says, pulling me close.

"Well, you'll stay at the house."

"I've got a room, don't be silly," she says, proceeding to Garrett and Sis on the other side of me.

My former high school English lit teacher led the graveside service. With elegance and grace, she asked the gathered to offer up a hand of applause for my mother's faith in Christ, hereby, I'm sure, paving Tina's way into the next world despite the top forty rundown inside the church.

I looked out over the hills of the sprawling green grounds of the cemetery, wondering if I would one day be planted here with Garrett, Sis, and Tina, or if I'd be burned and scattered over the Pacific or other parts unknown.

As Caroline whispers, "Why didn't you tell me your father was so handsome?" Jewel Ann and two other bluehairs say the service was interesting. Tina would have *loved* that.

❖

At the end of the longest day of my life, my father asked me to sleep with him. No fanfare, no hemming and hawing, just him showing up in the doorway of the bathroom as I'm washing my face for bed. "That's a mighty big bed in there without your mama. I mean, if you wanted to come take up the other half of it, I suppose that'd be all right."

Minutes later I'm lying next to him in the same spot Tina had taken for forty years, staring at the outline of the wobbly ceiling fan above us.

"I met her when she first moved to town," Garrett says, his deep voice cutting the silence of the night like a sneeze in church.

"We were thirteen. Class? Good God, boy, she was class all the way. I'd never even seen a green salad till she came on the scene."

As the movie of my prepubescent parents meeting cute plays in my head, my father's voice cracks with emotion. "I took her hand. I took her hand every night before we fell asleep."

Ten seconds pass before he reaches down and takes mine.

"You'll never know how much I worry about you," he says. "Neither you nor your sister can keep anybody. And I want to know there's somebody looking out for you out there. If I had my druthers, I'd want it to be a woman. But I just want you to find *somebody*."

I want so badly to turn and see what his face looks like when he says something so uncharacteristically progressive. But my eyes are frozen on the whirling blades of the ceiling fan.

"I had to take two ibuprofen for the headache," he says. "Too much crying, I guess. They're on the table next to you if you need 'em."

I stayed with my father for three months after that. He took my hand every night before we fell asleep.

THE DIXIE

February 4, 2002
<u>Crime</u> <u>Scene</u>

Jeans Burned

Gwen Gaylord, 55, was arrested Friday for starting a fire in city limits without a permit. Jackson Police Officer Oscola Turner said an inebriated Gaylord had used a can of gasoline and matches to set fire to a pair of Levi's she'd retrieved from her home on County Road 1 near Tidetown around eleven p.m. Turner quoted Gaylord as claiming she started the fire in the road in front of her residence because this particular pair of jeans would always remember. "Look, everyone has a bad day," Turner told *The Dixie*, "but the law's the law, and she broke it." Gaylord was released on Saturday after a brief psychological interview.

38

On the day I've finally chosen to return to California, I turn around in the carport and there, sitting next to my suitcase, is the ugliest Yorkie mix I've ever laid eyes on. Reaching carefully for my bag, I avoid any sudden movements as the last thing I can possibly stand is more drama. But to my complete and utter surprise, Puffy remains motionless, blinking her one good eye, as if the idea she'd ever do anyone bodily harm was ludicrous. Calling her bluff, I move my hands this way and that. Still, no reaction. I raise my arms Frankenstein-like above my head, but Puffy just scratches her chin, looking out over the last of the summer roses in the garden.

Sis embraces me in silence, pulling me so close I think she might break me in two. Fanny walks over and gives me a big, twisty hug. Looking past her shoulder, I can see my father just over the fence, methodically scooping dead poplar leaves from the pool's surface with the net. Fanny pats me on the arm and gently pushes me toward the rental car.

❖

On our way to the airport, the long, dark shadows of the ancient oaks stroke our faces like playful witches' hands as we drive through the streets of downtown Jackson. At one of the only red lights on Commerce Street, a boy around the age of ten races across the street, a clumsy sand-colored puppy on a leash charging ahead of him toward Quincey Drake's Hardware on the corner.

Squirming down in her seat, Caroline pulls a sweater around her arms. "Mind if I sleep till we get to the airport?"

"Go ahead," I say. I'd wondered if her coming out to retrieve me would feel like we were falling back into our routine, but the vibe was already different. We were two people who had moved on with our lives, but our bond would be forever sealed.

"Are you sure you're okay?"

"I'm fine," I say. "Sleep."

She touches my knee and lets the seat back.

"Good grief," I say, staring at the tall, unshaven fellow coming down the steps of Quincey's carrying a cardboard crate under one arm and stopping to finger one of the bright crimson garden tillers out front.

"What?" Caroline says, scooching up an inch.

Joe Tucker smiles and calls a greeting to the boy as he and his puppy disappear inside the hardware store.

"Is that him?" Caroline practically presses her nose to the passenger window.

"Yes."

Joe sets the crate down on the steps and picks up the handles of a tiller, steering the damned thing down some imaginary garden row.

"What are the odds?" she says.

"You could say the same thing about my entire trip, doll. It never ends."

"The light's green," Caroline says in a hushed, reverent tone, God love her. She lets her seat back up for a better view.

Over Joe's shoulder, I can make out the puppy sitting obediently next to the boy near the front counter just inside the store.

From behind, an impatient driver taps his horn three times

in succession, but as a veteran of rush hour traffic on the worst freeways imaginable, I am not easily moved. As the car behind me honks again, this time more urgently, Joe glances in our direction, a hint of recognition as he scrutinizes the inhabitants of the car causing the fracas on the otherwise bucolic street.

"I think he sees us," Caroline says.

Joe waves enthusiastically and motions us to pull over. I can feel my shoulders tightening up around my neck.

"Well, let's do this," she says, like a question.

Joe is now waving both his arms in the air.

Gripping the steering wheel with both hands, I hear a tiny voice inside me ask a childish, hypothetical question. If someone said I would have to relive every second of the past two and a half years if I could start on the day when Joe first hollered at me from the roof of his parents' house, would I?

"Come *on*, you're gonna pull over, aren't you?"

Before I can even attempt to, Joe approaches the car with a big excited grin, knocking once on the hood on his way over to my open window.

The top of my scalp begins to tingle, and the tension in my shoulders melts.

I ignore another irksome toot as an antique truck hauling bales of hay to one of the inland farms passes us from the other lane, flecks of dust and earth suspended in its wake.

Like a good Southern boy, I close my eyes, bow my head, and make a wish.

About the Author

Phillip Irwin Cooper's one-man-show, *Counting For Thunder*, ran for seven months in Los Angeles. Phillip starred in the film adaptation from Wolfe Releasing, a project he also directed, wrote, and produced. At its World Premiere at Rhode Island International Film Festival, *Counting For Thunder* took home the Jury Award for Best Alternative Feature. The film won Audience Awards at both Columbia Gorge International Film Festival and Fairhope Film Festival. Phillip lives in Santa Monica, California.

Books Available From Bold Strokes Books

Counting for Thunder by Phillip Irwin Cooper. A struggling actor returns to the Deep South to manage a family crisis but finds love and ultimately his own voice as his mother is regaining hers for possibly the last time. (978-1-63555-450-2)

Survivor's Guilt and Other Stories by Greg Herren. Award-winning author Greg Herren's short stories are finally pulled together into a single collection, including the Macavity Award–nominated title story and the first-ever Chanse MacLeod short story. (978-1-63555-413-7)

Saints + Sinners Anthology 2019, edited by Tracy Cunningham and Paul Willis. An anthology of short fiction featuring the finalist selections from the 2019 Saints + Sinners Literary Festival. (978-1-63555-447-2)

The Shape of the Earth by Gary Garth McCann. After appearing in *Best Gay Love Stories*, *HarringtonGMFQ*, *Q Review*, and *Off the Rocks*, Lenny and his partner Dave return in a hotbed of manhood and jealousy. (978-1-63555-391-8)

Exit Plans for Teenage Freaks by 'Nathan Burgoine. Cole always has a plan—especially for escaping his small-town reputation as "that kid who was kidnapped when he was four"—but when he teleports to a museum, it's time to face facts: it's possible he's a total freak after all. (978-1-163555-098-6)

Death Checks In by David S. Pederson. Despite Heath's promises to Alan to not get involved, Heath can't resist investigating a shopkeeper's murder in Chicago, which dashes their plans for a romantic weekend getaway. (978-1-163555-329-1)

Of Echoes Born by 'Nathan Burgoine. A collection of queer fantasy short stories set in Canada from Lambda Literary Award finalist 'Nathan Burgoine. (978-1-63555-096-2)

The Lurid Sea by Tom Cardamone. Cursed to spend eternity on his knees, Nerites is having the time of his life. (978-1-62639-911-2)

Sinister Justice by Steve Pickens. When a vigilante targets citizens of Jake Finnigan's hometown, Jake and his partner Sam fall under suspicion themselves as they investigate the murders. (978-1-63555-094-8)

Club Arcana: Operation Janus by Jon Wilson. Wizards, demons, Elder Gods: Who knew the universe was so crowded, and that they'd all be out to get Angus McAslan? (978-1-62639-969-3)

Triad Soul by 'Nathan Burgoine. Luc, Anders, and Curtis—vampire, demon, and wizard—must use their powers of blood, soul, and magic to defeat a murderer determined to turn their city into a battlefield. (978-1-62639-863-4)

Gatecrasher by Stephen Graham King. Aided by a high-tech thief, the Maverick Heart crew race against time to prevent a cadre of savage corporate mercenaries from seizing control of a revolutionary wormhole technology. (978-1-62639-936-5)

Wicked Frat Boy Ways by Todd Gregory. Beta Kappa brothers Brandon Benson and Phil Connor play an increasingly dangerous game of love, seduction, and emotional manipulation. (978-1-62639-671-5)

Death Goes Overboard by David S. Pederson. Heath Barrington and Alan Keyes are two sides of a steamy love triangle as they encounter gangsters, con men, murder, and more aboard an old lake steamer. (978-1-62639-907-5)

A Careful Heart by Ralph Josiah Bardsley. Be careful what you wish for...love changes everything. (978-1-62639-887-0)

Worms of Sin by Lyle Blake Smythers. A haunted mental asylum turned drug treatment facility exposes supernatural detective Finn M'Coul to an outbreak of murderous insanity, a strange parasite, and ghosts that seek sex with the living. (978-1-62639-823-8)

Tartarus by Eric Andrews-Katz. When Echidna, Mother of all Monsters, escapes from Tartarus and into the modern world, only an Olympian has the power to oppose her. (978-1-62639-746-0)

Rank by Richard Compson Sater. Rank means nothing to the heart, but the Air Force isn't as impartial. Every airman learns that rank has its privileges. What about love? (978-1-62639-845-0)

The Grim Reaper's Calling Card by Donald Webb. When Katsuro Tanaka begins investigating the disappearance of a young nurse, he discovers more missing persons, and they all have one thing in common: The Grim Reaper Tarot Card. (978-1-62639-748-4)

Smoldering Desires by C.E. Knipes. Evan McGarrity has found the man of his dreams in Sebastian Tantalos. When an old boyfriend from Sebastian's past enters the picture, Evan must fight for the man he loves. (978-1-62639-714-9)